ALSO BY AMBER D. LEWIS

RECOMMENDED READING ORDER

THE NIGHT THE STARS FELL

SCARS: ALAK'S STORY

A FIRE AND STARLIGHT NOVELLA

SCARS

Alak's Story

AMBER D. LEWIS

Print ISBN: 978-1-7370541-2-2

Ebook ISBN: 978-1-7370541-3-9

Cover Design and Formatting: Once Upon an Amber Dawn

Editor: Andi L. Gregory

For Business Inquiries visit www.amberdlewis.com or write to 4359 Wade Hampton Blvd, #282, Taylors, SC 29687

For all the broken hearts seeking to heal.
Life is worth living.

AUTHOR NOTE

This book contains mentions and acts of suicide, attempted suicide, and physical abuse. For more detailed information, please see the Content Warning Information page at the end of the book following the acknowledgments or visit https://www.amberdlewis.com/content-warnings.

US National Suicide Prevention Hotline:
1-800-273-8255

UK National Suicide Prevention Hotline:
0800 689 5652

Canada Suicide Prevention Service Call:
1-833-456-4566
Canada Suicide Prevention Service Text: 45645

Australia Suicide Callback Service:
1300 659 467
Australia Talk Suicide:
*https://suicidepreventionpathways.org.au/
make-a-referral*

ONE

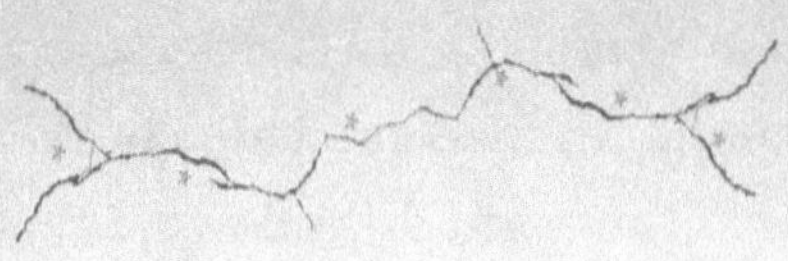

W hat have I told you, boy?" my father slurs, swinging his fists in my direction.

I duck, barely managing to escape. This infuriates him. He growls and lunges toward me, grabbing my shirt and jerking me closer. He slams his fist into my face, the metallic tang of blood flooding my mouth.

"Please, Da, stop," I plead, spitting blood onto the ground.

I beg, but I know from experience he won't listen. He never does. Instead, he laughs and takes another swing, this one grazing my chin. I manage to wiggle out of my shirt, leaving it in his hands. He's pissed enough that my actions confuse him for a moment, but once it registers what I've done, he's furious. And I'm cornered. His hands fumble for the nearby bottle, the one emptied in one sitting not long ago. He swings it, missing me but striking the wall. The glass shatters, spraying through the air. I throw my hands up, protecting my face, but shards of glass stick in my palms and chest.

"Look what you've done!" he roars. "Look at this mess!" He waves the jagged edges of the bottle inches from my face. I swallow and shrink back. "You'll clean this up, you little no-good bastard."

He strikes me again with the bottle, scraping the jagged edges of broken glass across my bare chest. It stings and I fight back tears as the blood drips down. I can't cry, though. Tears only give him strength. I clench my fists at my side.

"Stop," I choke out.

His eyes go wide as he laughs. "What's that boy?"

I swallow, clenching my fists even tighter to keep them from trembling. "I said 'stop.'"

His face grows stern. "You need some respect. That bitch of a mother you had didn't teach you any respect."

He swings the bottle and I duck. I'm not so lucky when he swings it again, the intact part of the bottle slamming against my temple. I slump to the ground, my head throbbing. My father looms over me, leering down. My vision is blurred, but I force myself to focus.

"I should just get rid of you. Nobody would miss you," he drawls. "Be doing the world a favor. You're nothing more than a worthless piece of shit."

He leans toward me and I kick up with my feet. He stumbles back, tripping over something behind him. He falls, his head catching the corner of a table. When he doesn't get up, I rise, unsteady, unsure. Blood pours from his head, pooling around him, his eyes open but unseeing. My heart thrums against my ribcage. I assume he's dead, but his hand twitches, making me jump. Terrified, I snatch a large broken shard of glass. As I slowly approach his body, my hand starts to shake uncontrollably.

"You'll never hurt me again," I mumble.

Without another thought, I plunge the shard of glass into his neck, slicing his throat. If he wasn't dead for sure before, he is now. What I've done washes over me, and I throw the glass down, staring at my blood-soaked hands in horror. What have I done?

I wake with a jerk. I lie still for a moment, breath hard and ragged. I drag my hand across my face. It's shaking. I wake shaking every time I have this dream, which is almost every night. Probably because it's more memory than dream. I sit up, shaking my head. I'm not a helpless ten-year-old anymore. It's been over four years since that incident. Almost five, actually, and no one has ever suspected me of anything to do with my father's death. No one cares about people like me.

I rise and stretch, rolling my neck as I look around. I fell asleep in another back alley. I sigh. Just another typical night. I stroll out into the street. It's already busy, but I guess a capital city like Embervein is always that way. I grin and my eyes light up. Plenty of people bustling around means more money. I stumble through the crowd, casually bumping into people here and there, snatching coin purses. I'm always a little baffled at how easy most people are to steal from. People are too trusting.

Smirking to myself, I head over to a small booth where a vendor is selling a selection of pastries. I study the options, my stomach rumbling. When was the last time I ate? The vendor eyes me suspiciously, so I pull a couple coins from my pocket so he can see I have money. He doesn't need to know it's stolen.

"I'll take a danish," I say, flipping the man a coin.

He grunts and allows me to take the pastry. Smiling, I scoop it up and take a bite. I munch my breakfast as I stroll down the busy street.

"Out of the way!" a voice booms, making people scuttle to the edges of the roadway. "Clear the road!"

I step to the side with the rest of the crowd, peering curiously down the street in the direction of the voice. A large man dressed in a sharp black and gold Guard uniform on a black horse leads a caravan. Behind the man are several other soldiers, following in neat lines, escorting a maroon and gold carriage with the royal crest on the doors. More soldiers march behind the carriage.

"Is it the prince?" a girl near me asks her friend, leaning forward.

"It must be! I heard he was leaving for Gleador today," her friend confirms.

More chatter and gossip explode around me, and I conclude that it is likely the crown prince in the carriage. When it passes directly in front of me, I'm a little disappointed to see the curtains are drawn. I've always wondered what the young prince looks like. We're almost the exact same age, just born into very different circumstances.

After the caravan passes through, most people spill into the road, going about their business. I have no real business to occupy me, so I follow the carriage. I'm not stupid enough to make it obvious what I'm doing. I skirt around the edges of the road, ducking behind buildings and carts, occasionally pausing, pretending to browse or talk to people.

I follow the procession to the edge of town. I'm considering how far I want to actually continue whatever it is I'm doing when the carriage comes to a halt outside the main gate. The Guard at the front rides past the other soldiers, dividing them up into groups, some of which ride on ahead. The others settle in closer to the carriage, surrounding it on all four sides, careful not to fall off the sloping sides of the road into the ditch.

As they rearrange their ranks, I notice an odd shadow cast under the carriage. At first I think I might've imagined it, but when I see a flash of blue, I'm positive something—or someone—is underneath. With a smirk, I sneak along the outer wall of the city, crossing over to the other side of the caravan for a better view. I patiently wait until the procession takes off again, the carriage bouncing down the road surrounded by soldiers. Once it's around the corner, mostly out of sight, I make my way down to the road. Off to the side at the bottom of the incline I see two boys. The taller of the two is wearing a sharp soldier's uniform and scowling, but the other is laughing while he switches out his blue and gold tunic for more casual clothes.

"Hurry up, Bram," the slighter of the two says, grinning. "Change. We need to get off the side of the road before someone sees us."

"We need to get you back in that carriage," the other grumbles, his scowl deepening, but he starts to change from his uniform anyway.

The younger boy, who I am now positive is Prince Ehren,

runs his hand through his neatly combed brown hair, tousling it. His guard, Bram, rolls his eyes.

"You need to loosen up!" Ehren laughs. "It's not often we get a day off!"

"Day off?" Bram huffs. "How is following you around making sure you don't do anything stupid a day off for me?"

Ehren scoffs. "Come now, I'm not that bad."

"Your father is going to have my head when he realizes what you did," Bram sighs. "If anything happens to you while you are avoiding your responsibilities, I will be in even worse trouble."

"How long before they realize I'm missing, do you think?" the prince muses, holding up a hand to shield his eyes from the sun as he peers down the road after the disappearing carriage.

"Well," Bram considers, stuffing his uniform in a bag on the ground. "If they are smart they will check to see if you are still in the carriage within the hour."

Ehren grins. "They're not that smart."

Bram sighs. "Unfortunately, you are probably right. I give them two or three hours at the earliest, but likely closer to four."

This seems like the perfect time to enter into their conversation. I saunter over to the edge of the road and grin down at them.

"Unless someone were to go tell them right now," I say, both of them spinning to face me.

The soldier grabs his sword up from where he's tossed it on the ground and points it in my direction, though I'm well out of range. "Who are you?"

I bow. "Alak Dunne at your service."

Ehren cocks his head, studying me, amusement twinkling in his sea-green eyes. Bram seems far less amused.

"And what, Mr. Alak Dunne, do you want in exchange for your silence?" Ehren asks, crossing his arms as a smile plays at the corners of his lips.

Bram's eyes widen, and he looks at the prince in disbelief. "You don't negotiate with people like this!"

"Oh, so we're going to—what? Run him through with your sword, and then leave his body on the side of the road?"

Bram shrugs. "That works for me."

Ehren rolls his eyes and starts walking toward me.

"Ehren! What the hell do you think you are doing?" Bram cries, scrambling after him.

Ehren climbs up onto the road and stands a couple feet away, his eyes still studying me. I grin.

"Well, what do you want for your silence?" Ehren asks at length as a scowling Bram comes up behind him, his sword still out. "Money? I have money. Jewels? Though you don't look like much of a jewel person. How about a change of clothes and a good meal? Maybe a place to sleep the night that isn't a gutter or back alley?"

I struggle to keep my face neutral. I don't want him to know he struck a chord. I'm obviously little more than a street urchin, and he knows it. He knows I sleep in the streets and steal to survive. I'm worthless and pathetic. I pretend, instead, to weigh his words like I actually have something to offer. Like I am worth something. I've become quite good at pretending I'm someone I'm not.

"Twenty gold markes and new clothes," I say at length.

"Deal!" The prince grins. "But I don't have that much on me right now."

"Gods' sake, Ehren," Bram sighs, sheathing his sword. "Did you forget your money again?"

Ehren grins sheepishly. "There is an excellent possibility that's what happened."

I laugh. Before I even realize what I'm saying, I find myself adjusting my terms. "How about instead of the money, you spend the day with me?"

Once I've said the words out loud, I realize how stupid they sound, and I can't keep the slight flush from my cheeks. I wait for them to laugh at the desperate street boy, but Ehren only cocks his head, studying me for a minute, no judgement in his eyes.

"All right, then," he replies, drawing out the words. My heart stops as a grin spreads across his face. "It might actually be nice to have someone aid my shenanigans instead of trying to prevent them."

Bram sighs and presses his fingers to his temples. "I want a raise."

"You deserve one," Ehren says with a shrug. "Well, shall we be off?"

I grin, feeling oddly nervous. "What's the plan, mate?"

"Hm . . . ," Ehren muses, placing a finger to his chin. "How about we start with a pint or two at the tavern?"

"You are not even fifteen!" Bram cries in disbelief.

"I'll be fifteen in two days," Ehren argues, rolling his eyes.

I didn't realize we were really that close in age. I turned fifteen not quite two weeks ago.

"And that still puts you a year short of sixteen, which,

may I remind you, is the age taverns are allowed to serve you," Bram says sharply.

Ehren grins, eyes sparkling. "Ah, but they don't have to know I'm only fifteen."

"You are the gods' damned prince, Ehren," Bram spits. "They will most surely recognize you and know exactly who you are, and therefore how old you are, the second you walk through the door."

"You're sixteen," Ehren says pointedly. "You could—"

"No."

"But, Bram—"

"I said no."

"I can get the drinks," I cut in.

Both pairs of eyes turn to me. Bram's are set in a firm scowl, but Ehren's are wide and bright.

"You're sixteen?" Ehren asks cheerily.

I shrug, grinning. "Do I look sixteen?"

Ehren enthusiastically says, "Yes!" at the same time Bram shakes his head replying, "No."

I laugh. "Technically, I'm only fifteen." Ehren's face falls, but I continue. "But that's never stopped me before. Give me the coins, and I guarantee I can get you drinks."

Ehren turns to Bram and grins, motioning toward me. "Well, give him money."

Bram's eyes narrow at Ehren. "You're insufferable, you know that, right?"

"That's why you love me."

Bram rolls his eyes, but he doesn't argue. He reaches inside his pocket, pulling out a few coins. He hesitates before handing them to me. "You run off with this money, and I will hunt you down."

My eyes go wide and I swallow, nodding. "I swear to you, mate. I'll bring you drinks." I glance around. "Are you going to sit on the side of the road and wait for me?"

"No, I want to see the town," Ehren says, strolling toward the city behind us.

"Are you sure that's a good idea?" Bram asks, following him.

"I didn't escape to sit on the side of the road," Ehren replies as I fall into stride beside him.

Bram leaps ahead of Ehren and holds out his hands, palms forward. "Ehren! Stop! Think about what you are suggesting. You go back into town, and you will almost surely get caught."

Ehren waves him off and pushes on past Bram. "Eh, I'll be busted sooner or later anyway, so I might as well have some fun in the meantime." He glances at me. "Now, how about those drinks?"

I'm not all that familiar with Embervein, so I allow Ehren to lead the way. We take several wrong turns before we finally get to the tavern most likely to serve someone my age. Ehren and Bram take up residence in the back alley while I wander inside. It's unusually crowded for mid-morning. My eyes dart around and I swallow. Maybe I've made a mistake. After a moment of hesitation, I shake off my doubts and approach the counter. This isn't the first time I've done something like this. A sturdy man with dark hair and a stubble covered face stands directly behind the bar, wiping a mug with a rag.

"What do you need, boy?" the man grunts, not even bothering to look up.

"I was wondering if I could get three ales, please?" I say,

putting on my most charming smile as I slap Bram's coins on the counter.

The man barely glances up from the mug, arching an eyebrow. "How old are you, boy?"

"Seventeen!" I reply, grinning.

The man huffs and looks back at the mug. "I don't have time for your nonsense today. Get on with you."

I open my mouth to try again, but I can tell there'd be no point. There's no way this man is going to let me buy one drink, let alone three. So, that means buying them is out of the question. Time for Plan B.

I turn around and inspect the other patrons. There are about twenty others clustered around the tables in the tavern. The largest cluster is a group of seven young men in the far back corner, not much older than myself. Judging by their crisp, bright clothes, they come from money. Since we're in the capital, it's highly likely they're nobility of some sort. Judging by how loud they are and the number of empty mugs and bottles scattered across the table, they've been drinking for a while now and are probably properly pissed, despite the fact it's not even noon. I grin, approaching their table.

"Pardon me," I say to the blond on the end. He looks up at me and scowls.

"Who are you and what do you want?" I smell a lot of alcohol on his breath. He's the perfect mark. I bite back my grin.

"Oh, sorry. I thought you were someone else." I start to turn and walk away when the boy calls out to me.

"Wait, who'd you think I was?"

I turn to him, grimacing. "Well, this is terribly awkward."

"Awkward?" he asks, arching his eyebrows. "What's awkward?"

I glance around before leaning in closer to whisper, "I thought you were a young woman I'm meant to meet here."

The words take a moment to register, but I can tell the moment he makes sense of them. The boy's face turns bright red as his friends snicker.

"Excuse me?!"

I throw my hands up defensively. "It's my mistake." I lean in closer and whisper, "It's just that, well, that fellow there"—I motion quickly to his friend sitting the farthest from him— "said he would be with a lovely blonde young lady here at the pub at this time and that she would sit in your exact seat. He promised she'd be, well, easy, and I figured, why not." I end with a shrug as the boy's face grows redder.

The boy spins to face his friend, who's currently laughing at his expense. "What the hell, Braxton!"

The boy, Braxton, I suppose, widens his eyes. "What?"

"Don't you 'what' me!" the first boy yells. The others now eye both friends with drunken delight, interest piqued. "Did you tell this stranger that you would hook him up with a girl this afternoon, and then brought me along as a joke? Your pranks are getting old."

Braxton's eyes grow wider as he shakes his head. "No! I'd never do that!"

"I think maybe he meant to bring your sister. Do you have a sister?" I ask, cautiously. "He acted quite positively like there'd be a girl."

If the boy was mad before, he's seething now. "Is that why you were asking about Rebecca earlier? Why you wanted her to come along?"

I try my best to hide my smile. To be honest, I'm surprised this is working. The sister idea was a shot in the dark at best. I suppose I'm lucky these boys have been drinking long enough that their inhibitions are down, their common sense faded to practically nothing.

"Hey, you know I'd never pawn Rebecca off on someone!"

"Why?" the first boy spits. "Saving her for yourself?"

"Yes! I mean, no! No!"

Without warning, the blond boy lunges across the table, grabbing the other boy by his shirt.

"Oi! Stop that!" the bartender calls out.

When the boys don't pay him any attention and keep squabbling, knocking over a tankard of ale, the bartender sighs and shuffles across the room to break up the fight. I quickly scamper over and duck behind the bar. Nerves swell, but I keep my hands steady as I grab the nearest bottle I can find. I slide out from behind the counter, barely avoiding detection. Instead of going out the front door, I wind around out the back, sneaking into the back alley where Bram and Ehren wait expectantly. As I approach, Ehren grins, but Bram actually looks upset I succeeded.

"I knew you could do it!" Ehren exclaims, clapping me on the shoulder with one hand as he takes the bottle with the other.

Bram scowls and yanks the bottle from Ehren, scrutinizing it.

"It's not poison, mate," I laugh.

"Who cares?" Ehren mumbles, grabbing it back and popping the cork with his teeth.

He throws his head back, taking a big gulp. He wipes red liquid from his mouth, passing the bottle to me, so I can take a swig. The bottle I grabbed is apparently cherry mead, and it's not half bad. It's stronger than what I'm used to, so it doesn't take long before I'm feeling a bit tipsy. Judging by the way Ehren keeps giggling, he's also feeling the effects. Bram at least has the common sense to only drink a few sips, even though he's the only one of us old enough to have purchased the mead in the first place.

"You should really stop drinking that," Bram scolds, scowling.

"No," Ehren slurs, tipping back the bottle and gulping more.

"Ehren," Bram says, authority ringing in his voice. Ehren pulls the bottle back and sticks his tongue out at Bram.

"You take all the fun out of fun things," Ehren complains and I laugh.

Bram switches his scowl to me, making me laugh harder. Ehren starts to pass the bottle back, but Bram knocks it from his hand. The bottle crashes to the ground, shattering and spilling what remains of the mead. As my eyes focus on the broken shards of red-drenched glass, my heart stops.

No, it's not blood. I tell myself, taking a shuddering breath. *It's not blood. It's mead. It's only broken glass. No one is coming for you. No one knows. No one can hurt you anymore. You're safe. It's not blood.*

"Hey, are you okay?"

I jerk my gaze away from the broken bottle to Ehren,

who's watching me, deep concern on his face.

"Oh, uh, yeah," I fumble, forcing a smile and shoving my hands in my pockets. "I'm right as rain, mate."

Bram folds his arms and eyes me, scowling. "I think you had too much to drink."

I nod. "Aye. Probably."

I'm tired of their judging, assessing gazes. I glance down the alley toward the busy city.

"So, what are your plans, now that you've had your drinks?" I ask nonchalantly, eager to shift their focus on something besides me.

"I don't know," Ehren muses. He turns to Bram, "What do you think?"

"What do I think?" Bram asks. "I think we should go back to the castle and tell your father you skipped out. It may not be too late to fix this."

Ehren shakes his head firmly. "Nope. That is not going to happen. I want to have fun."

"We could find some girls . . . ," I drawl as their eyes turn to me.

Ehren grins. "Girls? Now I like that . . ."

"No," Bram says firmly, shaking his head and glaring at me. "That is a definite no."

"Aw, come on, Bram!" Ehren whines, slurring his words slightly.

He must've had more to drink than I thought. Or he's really bad at holding his alcohol. Or he's exaggerating for effect. Whatever the reason, Bram notices, too.

"You are drunk. We need to keep you out of harm's way," Bram says, watching Ehren lean against the wall.

"Then you better not take me back to the palace. If my

father sees me drunk, it's your head," Ehren points out with a mischievous grin. Oh! I like this prince.

Bram sighs. "Valid point."

"I know a place we could go," I suggest.

Bram's eyes turn to me. "Where? And if you suggest a whorehouse . . ."

I laugh. "No, nothing like that, mate. I was going to suggest the nearby forest. I doubt anyone would look there for him."

"No," Ehren argues. "I told you, I want to have fun. There's nothing fun in a forest."

"We could swim," I say with a shrug.

Ehren squints up at the sun. "It is hot today."

Bram sighs, looking from Ehren to me and back again. Finally, he throws his hands in the air. "Fine. If we have to do something, that seems better than most other options you would be likely to suggest."

Ehren staggers away from the wall, grinning. "Let's go!"

He charges down the alley, and I follow, laughing. Bram trips along behind us. As we spill onto the main street, Ehren ducks his head down, trying to make himself less noticeable. We cross several streets, going undetected. We're almost out of the city when someone calls after us.

"Hey! You! It's you!"

I turn to see the blond boy from earlier marching toward me, seething.

"Nope. Not me, mate. Got the wrong fella," I say, spinning away and chasing after Ehren and Bram.

The boy catches up to me and grabs my arm, jerking me back with enough force I wince. "No, it was you! You got us kicked out of The Gilded Goblet!"

"Are you sure it was me and not some other extremely handsome boy?" I ask, trying to wiggle from his grasp. This arsehole is surprisingly strong.

"No," he insists. "It was most definitely you. You ruined my day, and now I'm going to ruin yours."

He takes a swing at me, but I've had plenty of experience dodging flying fists. It also helps that he's bloody pissed and I'm not. But he's not alone. One of his friends takes a swing at me next, and his fist smashes against my lip, filling my mouth with blood. My stomach turns. Gods, how I hate the taste and smell of blood.

"Stop it!" Ehren yells from behind me as I spit blood onto the ground. "Stop it, Dylan! Let him go!"

My attacker, Dylan, pauses and looks past me to Ehren. I hear Bram mumble, "What are you doing, you idiot," but Ehren lunges forward anyway, pulling me from Dylan's grasp. Dylan's eyes focus on Ehren in a confused scowl.

"Y-you're supposed to be gone," Dylan slurs.

"Surprise!" Ehren grins. "Why're you ganging up on this guy, anyway?"

Dylan scowls along with his other friends. "We're teaching this loser a lesson. He got us kicked out of the tavern."

"Are you sure you didn't get kicked out for drinking too much? I can smell the alcohol from here," Ehren mumbles.

"It does seem a little unfair that it is seven of you against this one boy," Bram muses. "Are you all that unskilled?"

Wait. Are they defending me? Are they actually helping me? Why aren't they running? They should be long gone by now, leaving me to deal with seven boys by myself.

Dylan's eyes flash. "I have plenty of skill."

Ehren waves him off. "Then go impress someone else."

Dylan clenches his fists by his sides. "Not until I teach this boy a lesson."

"Holy shit!" Ehren cries, looking past the group of boys, his eyes going wide. "What the hell is that?"

All the boys spin around while Dylan asks, "What?"

Ehren grabs my arm, pulling me after him while he whisper-yells, "Run!"

My feet stumble into a run behind Bram and Ehren. It only takes a minute before Dylan and his friends are in pursuit. We race through the busy street, people and animals diving out of our way as we jump over baskets and boxes, knocking over the occasional display. I'm regretting the alcohol in my system, but manage to fight its effects, as does Ehren. We have enough of a head start and less mead in our systems, so we're able to outrun Dylan and his comrades after a few minutes. We end up in a faraway alley on the edge of the city. Ehren collapses against the wall grinning wildly.

"Well, that was fun!"

Bram scowls and turns to me, breathing heavy from the run. "What exactly did you do to them?"

With a shrug, I quickly relay the story of how I managed to get the bottle of mead. Ehren bursts out laughing. I expect Bram to scold me, but he smiles instead.

"That was a risky ploy," Bram says slowly, "but I cannot deny I like seeing those bastards put at an inconvenience."

"Seems like we picked a good friend for the day," Ehren says with a wink.

Friend? Is that how they see me? But I don't have friends. I'm meant to be alone.

TWO

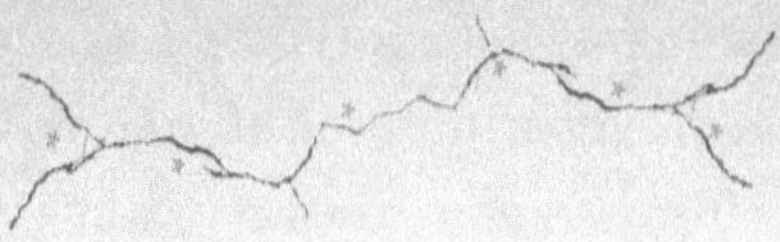

So," Ehren drawls, looking up at the city wall behind him. "Think we can climb this wall and get out of here?"

I shake my head. "You probably can't climb the wall, but you can climb up onto the roof of this building and leap across and off the wall." I gesture to the building to our left.

Bram scowls, and Ehren's eyes go wide. "What? You want me to jump from that roof to the wall?"

I look up. It's a distance of about three or four feet. I nod. "Yeah, mate. It's not as hard as it looks." The other two exchange a look, and I laugh. "Have I led you wrong yet?"

Bram is especially wary as they follow me up onto the roof via a wobbly stack of crates. I stand at the edge and look across to the wall. A nervous pit swells in my stomach. As casual as I might have made it sound, it isn't actually that easy. The wall is, at best, two feet thick—easy to miss or overshoot. I know what a broken arm feels like from not making a jump like this. I take a running leap before I can talk myself out of it. I'm almost surprised when my feet land squarely on the wall. I turn and face Bram and Ehren, throwing my arms in the air, victorious. Ehren licks his lips and starts to run, but Bram grabs his arm.

"Are you sure about this?" he asks, scowling. I wonder if he's always scowling. "There are at least a dozen ways out of the city that don't involve jumping off twelve-foot walls."

Ehren looks from Bram to me. I give him two thumbs up, and he grins. "I'm doing this!"

Bram releases Ehren's arm with a long sigh. Ehren takes off running, leaping from the edge of the roof. One foot lands on the wall, but the other misses. I quickly reach out and grab Ehren, pulling him onto the wall with me. We both almost tumble off but regain our balance. My heart races.

"Shit," Ehren mumbles, looking down at the ground. "That was close."

We look back over to Bram, who shakes his head. Ehren cups his hands around his mouth and yells, "Come on, Bram! You can do it!"

Still shaking his head, Bram runs and leaps with extraordinary skill and grace, landing flawlessly on the wall.

"You've done that before," I say, narrowing my eyes at him.

Bram smiles smugly but doesn't say anything to the contrary.

"Well, what now?" Ehren asks, putting his hands on his hips and looking down on the other side of the wall.

"Now"—I grin wickedly—"we jump."

Ehren spins to me. "We do what now?"

My grin widens. "We jump down off the wall.

Remember to bend your knees as you land, or you'll break your legs."

Ehren glances at Bram who shrugs. "What did you expect?"

Ehren turns back to me and crosses his arms, raising his eyebrows in a challenge. "Fine. You do it first."

I take a deep breath and leap. Judging by the swear words that slip from Ehren's mouth, I don't think he was expecting me to jump immediately. I land in a crouch and stand, looking back up at Ehren and Bram above me.

"See?" I call up to them. "Easy!"

Ehren turns and says something to Bram, but I can't hear it all the way down at the bottom of the wall. Bram shrugs. I wonder if they're planning on leaving when Ehren takes the leap. He falls to the ground, tumbling away. He rolls over, lying on his back.

"Are you okay?" I ask, standing over him.

"I think so," he says as a grin spreads across his face.

Bram lands next to me with the dexterity of a cat before standing and offering his hand to the prince. Ehren clasps Bram's hand and is pulled to his feet. Ehren brushes grass and dirt off his clothes, still grinning.

"Well, we didn't die, so that is something," Bram mumbles.

"Let's go swim, then!" I say. "Last one there has to swim entirely naked."

"You're on!" Ehren crows, taking off.

The three of us race to the nearby forest. Bram is clearly the most skilled of the three of us, but he won't take the full lead because he's constantly watching Ehren. Even now, he won't let his guard down. He's too loyal. Ehren also has plenty of training, and his stamina exceeds mine. I'm the last into the trees by a good bit.

Bram seems to know the forest the best and leads the way to the water. When we reach the trickling stream we move along the edge for a few minutes until we find a section that's deep enough for swimming. Ehren and Bram quickly shed their outer layers and get down to their underwear. When I get down to mine, I hesitate.

"Well, mates," I mumble. "I was the last into the forest, so I guess that means I swim naked."

"No!" Ehren cries out, holding up his hands, blocking me from his view as he laughs. "We'll allow you to remain clothed."

"Are you sure?" I ask, grinning. "Because rules are rules."

"We will allow it," Bram confirms, a hint of a smile on his lips.

I sigh and wade into the water. "Good. I wouldn't want you two to feel inadequate."

"Excuse me?" Ehren laughs. "I am far from inadequate! I'll show you!"

He makes to pull off his underpants, but Bram splashes water in his face. "Have some self-respect, Ehren!"

Ehren laughs, splashing Bram back. The next thing I know we're all splashing each other, laughing. We splash and play and swim for hours. I don't even mind the hungry pit in my stomach. I'm used to it. When we do finally climb from the water, soaked and a little sunburnt, we lie mostly naked on the bank. I feel Ehren's eyes on me, and I look over. He glances away, his cheeks reddening slightly.

"What?" I demand, a little harsher than I mean to.

"Nothing," Ehren mutters. "I just . . . I noticed your scars. That's all."

"Oh." I go silent and look back up at the trees above me. "Yeah. My scars."

Now Bram is looking at my bare chest, scowling.

"Look, mate, you keep looking at me like that, you're going to have to buy me a drink."

Bram shakes his head. "Who did that to you?"

I laugh bitterly and push up onto my elbows. "My father."

"Why?" Ehren asks, eyes wide.

"Because he hated me, I guess. But I'd rather not talk about him. He's not worth wasting breath on."

Bram nods. "How about we find some berries to eat? There should be some around here."

We all stand and search for food. We find several berry bushes, and we eat our fill, sticky, purple-red juice dripping down our chins. We are debating going back in the water when bells start ringing in the city.

"Shit," Ehren mumbles. "They've discovered I'm missing. I was hoping to get a few more hours of freedom. I guess the guards were smarter than I gave them credit."

"Do you have to go back now?" I ask, trying to hide my disappointment.

Bram nods. "If they follow usual protocol, search parties of soldiers will be swarming the city and surrounding areas soon."

"Oh," I concede. "Well, I suppose now it's time to get you back into the city."

"You're coming with us, right?" Ehren asks, eyes studying me.

I hesitate. "Well, I mean, I have to go back into the city eventually. I have a horse. I can't leave her."

"But you'll come with us, right?" Ehren presses.

I glance from Ehren to Bram. "I mean, I can."

Bram shrugs. "Why not?"

"Really?" I ask, my eyes going wide.

Bram nods. "I think we can make you into part of our cover story. Get dressed and we will head back into the city."

A smile creeps onto my lips, and I quickly turn to hide it. I pull on my clothes, heart racing. Is this what it might be like to have friends? Or will this "cover story" have me end up in the dungeon for kidnapping the prince? My heart sinks. That must be it. Why else would they want me around longer? Maybe once we get inside the gate, I'll split. I'll get Fawn and ride off before they can find me again.

With a sigh, I follow Bram and Ehren out of the woods toward the front gate of the city. I stay aware of my surroundings, ready to make a run for it. I need to wait for the right opportunity. At the gate soldiers flood out, surrounding us. My heart starts racing. I can't escape with this many soldiers. I'm trapped.

"My, my," Ehren says, grinning. "What an escort service. Are we going to form a parade? If so, I want a horse. And a crown."

"Your Majesty," says a soldier—a captain maybe? "We have orders to take you directly to your father."

The king. I'm going to be dragged in front of the king. This is how I die, isn't it?

Ehren doesn't seem bothered. He waves his hand. "So be it. Lead the way."

Surrounded by a horde of soldiers, we're escorted into

the castle. Everything is so clean and shiny. Portraits of royals and nobles line almost every hallway and corridor, and everything seems to be in shades of maroon, black, and gold. When we're finally pushed through the door into the throne room I gasp. It's so grand and ostentatious. Blood red marble coats the floor and obsidian columns rise like shadow giants. The king sits on a golden throne, glaring down at us. I suddenly find it hard to breathe.

"What exactly were you thinking?" the king roars and I wince.

"I had to help this poor boy, Father," Ehren replies, placing his hand on my shoulder, seemingly unphased.

The king arches his eyebrows. "What? How is that boy more important than you going to Gleador to help seal our alliance?"

"Well," Ehren replies, his voice dripping with feigned innocence. "We were leaving the city, and I looked out of my carriage window and saw this poor boy stuck in a ditch. He was lying unconscious. I think he must have been robbed." Ehren glances at me, giving me a nudge. "Right?"

"Oh, uh, right," I mumble. I look up at the king and then immediately bow my head. "I mean, yes, Your Majesty. Bandits attacked me outside the city. Your son was very kind and came to my aid."

Ehren turns back to his father, grinning. "It's not my fault that your soldiers didn't see me exit the carriage to help the boy. Only Bramfield here was able to assist me. I was so distracted with my good deed I didn't even notice the carriage ride off."

Ehren is grinning smugly, but his father is clearly less

than convinced. "And why did you not immediately return to the palace once you realized the carriage was gone?"

This question seems to stump Ehren. He opens his mouth, only to close it a second later.

"That was my fault, Your Majesty," Bram says, taking a step forward. "I was afraid that the bandits might still be nearby and thought it best we hide out for a little while to ensure we were not harmed."

The king narrows his eyes. I don't think he believes a single word, but at length, he says, "This trip will be rescheduled. You will go to Gleador. You will meet Princess Elaine."

Ehren's eyes gleam as he bows. "Yes, father."

The king surveys us another moment before waving his hand. "Dismissed."

Ehren spins on his heel and exits the throne room, Bram directly behind him. I trip after them. I stick as close as I can to Ehren and Bram as we weave through the castle. I have no idea where we're going or if they even want me along, but I have little choice. We finally come to a room and enter. It's a large room filled with chairs, couches, tables, and books with more rooms off the main one. I'm staring around in awe when Ehren turns to me.

"I'm glad we ran into you! You helped make quite the convincing story," he grins.

"Your father didn't believe a single bit of your lie," Bram counters, shutting the door.

Ehren shrugs. "Probably not. But I'm alive and not in a carriage headed to Gleador to be tricked into marriage, so I'm calling this a win."

Ehren must realize that I'm still staring around the room

because he turns to me. "Why do you look so flabbergasted?"

I shake my head, "I don't know. I've never been in a palace before. What room is this?"

Ehren cocks his head and grins. "This is my room. Well, part of it. The bed's through there." He gestures to one of the side rooms.

My eyes go wide. "All of this is your personal space?"

"Yep!" Ehren laughs. "I know it's a bit much, but I am a prince after all." He snaps his fingers. "I almost forgot, I promised you clothes and a place to sleep if you got me drinks and you followed through."

I shake my head and wave him off. "Unnecessary, mate. We amended the terms, remember?"

"No, I always follow through on my promises," Ehren says, crossing over into one of the side rooms. "I'm sure I have something that you can wear," he calls, his voice slightly muffled. "We look like we're about the same size." He reenters the main room a few moments later, arms laden with clothes. My eyes go wide as he dumps them in my arms.

"I . . . I can't accept these," I mumble.

"Please. I have more than I need, and I'm guessing you have the clothes on your back and nothing more. They're all yours. You can go right through there, into my dressing room, and change if you want privacy."

I nod and stumble into the dressing room. My dirty rags fall to the floor, and I pull on the discarded clothes of a prince. They're so soft and comfortable. I look up, catching my reflection in a mirror. I look like a different person.

When I go back into the other room Ehren smiles. "You look good!"

I find myself blushing, and Ehren waves his hands, his own cheeks turning a slight shade of pink. "I didn't mean that in a way like I think you look good like I want to, you know . . ."

I laugh. "Don't worry, mate. You're not my type." Ehren relaxes a bit. I glance over at Bram and add, "I prefer brown eyes, myself."

Ehren barks out a laugh while Bram flushes deeply, looking very uncomfortable.

"I like women," he blurts.

"Do you?" Ehren asks, arching an eyebrow. "Because not once have I seen you talk to one willingly besides your sister and mine."

Bram glares at Ehren, his cheeks still red. "I will find a girl one day. I don't see any point in wasting time flirting with every girl I see when I know I won't settle down with her. One day, I will find the girl I am meant to marry."

Ehren rolls his eyes. "You know, you can talk to a girl without wanting to marry her. Hell, you can even kiss a girl with no intention of marriage. You can even—"

"I get it!" Bram cuts Ehren off, his cheeks flushed a deep crimson, shaking his head. "When I kiss a girl, I want it to be love, not lust." He scowls and looks up at Ehren. "Why are we even talking about this right now?"

Ehren shrugs. "We were trying to figure out Alak's type, and apparently you are exactly his type."

I shake my head. "Naw, he's too uptight." Ehren laughs and Bram scowls. I laugh. "And I do tend to prefer women, I think, so you're both safe." I wink at them.

"Good to know!" Ehren grins. "Since you'll probably be sleeping here in my room with me."

"What?" Bram and I say together.

Ehren shrugs. "Why not? I have plenty of couches." He motions to the furniture around us, and I have to agree. "I doubt my father will allow a room to be prepared for you, so unless you want to sleep on the street again, you might as well sleep in here."

My heart is pounding in my chest as I take in the room. Me? Stay here in the palace? In the living quarters of the crown prince? It's too good to be true. Bram is eyeing me suspiciously, and I have a feeling he agrees.

"Ehren, maybe we should discuss this," Bram says slowly.

Ehren looks at Bram sharply. "There's nothing to discuss."

Bram sighs and pinches the bridge of his nose. "Ehren..."

"How about I get out of your way for a bit," I cut in. "I need to go check on my horse."

"Bring her to the royal stables," Ehren suggests, ignoring Bram.

"Really?" I ask. "I can bring her to the stables?"

Ehren nods. "Of course!"

Bram opens his mouth to argue, but I give Ehren a thankful nod and skirt out of the room before Bram can say anything. I'm sure the second the door closes behind me, Ehren and Bram will be arguing. There's a good chance when I return I may not have a place to stay the night, but right now I don't care. The fact that someone wants me around is something I've grown not to expect from anybody.

THREE

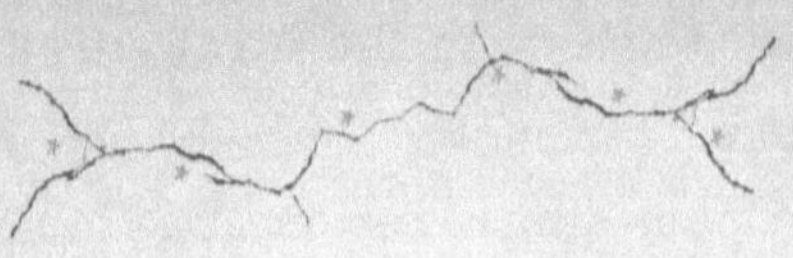

It takes longer than I anticipate to navigate through the castle and weave my way outside. Once I do, it doesn't take me long to find Fawn. She greets me with a happy huff as I approach her

"Hey, girl," I whisper, rubbing her nose. "Sorry I've left you for so long but, gods, do I have a story to tell you."

As I lead Fawn through the town, I tell her about my day. In the past few years, she's been my only companion, my only friend. When we approach the stables, a young boy with blond hair rushes out to meet us. He can't be more than six or seven years old.

"Are you the stable boy?" I ask, narrowing my eyes.

The boy nods, eyes wide with fear. "Me and my brother, Mark. But he's out running the horses right now. He's teaching me how to do everything on my own, though. I can help you, Sir. My name's Peter."

Sir. Well, that's new. I look down at the boy and see an eagerness in his eyes.

"Are you good with horses?" I ask, raising an eyebrow.

He nods. "I like them and they like me."

I smile and he relaxes. "Well, this is Fawn. She's very special to me. Can you take good care of her while I'm staying at the palace?"

The boy smiles and bobs his head up and down in an eager nod. "I can!"

My stomach drops a little as I hand the reins to the boy. I don't like being apart from Fawn, but the horses here are all taken care of. I'm sure I have nothing to worry about.

"What a beautiful horse!" a voice gasps from behind me.

I spin around and my breath catches as my heart leaps into my throat. Standing in front of me is the most beautiful girl I've ever seen. She has long, chestnut brown hair and gentle curves. She's leading a dapple-gray horse.

She walks up to me and strokes Fawn. "Is she yours?"

She looks at me, and I notice little specks of gold mixed into the brown of her eyes. I nod and manage to find my voice. "Aye, her name is Fawn."

"Fawn," she purrs, giving her another pat. "You're beautiful, Fawn."

"You, uh, like horses, love?"

She turns her sparkling eyes back to me.

"I do. I've always loved horses."

"Your horse is quite nice," I say, nodding to the horse she's leading.

"Oh, Solomon belongs to my brother," she says, waving her hand. "I usually borrow him or one of the other horses if Solomon isn't available. I don't have a horse of my own yet."

"Does he need food?" the young stable boy cuts in, taking Solomon's reins from the girl.

"Please," she says. "And plenty of water."

The boy nods and leads both horses off, leaving us alone together. Strange nerves flutter in my chest as the girl turns her bright eyes to me.

"Are you staying in the palace? If so, maybe we can walk back in together?"

I can't hide my smile. "Aye, I would enjoy that very much." I give her a little bow. "Alak Dunne at your service."

She grins and inclines her head. "Isabella Bramfield. Pleased to make your acquaintance."

I awkwardly offer her my arm, wondering if I'm doing this correctly. I've only ever seen others do it. But she doesn't hesitate to loop her arm through mine, so I must have done it right. My heart flutters at her touch.

As we walk, a thought strikes me. "Wait, Bramfield? Is your brother one of the prince's guard detail?"

"Ah, so you know my brother," she muses. "Interesting. I know he doesn't care for many of the nobles, so I apologize if you're—"

"Oh, no," I cut her off. "I'm not a noble."

"Oh?" She arches an eyebrow. "I assumed with your clothes . . ." She nods at the prince's hand-me-downs.

"Ah, yes." How do I explain this? "I, well, I very recently met your brother, and the prince, and they've kind of taken me under their wings."

It's a lame excuse. A horrible reason. But she accepts it with a nod and a smile.

"Good. Then that means we will hopefully be together a good bit."

She smiles and my heart threatens to beat from my chest. I want to spend every day of the rest of my life in the warmth from that smile. I offer her a smile of my own. "I would like that very much."

We walk side by side in silence for several steps, but as we enter the palace, I turn to her, finding my voice. "Would you like me to take you to your brother? He was with the prince last I saw him."

She shakes her head. "No. I'm heading to the library. Winnie—well, Princess Cadewynn—is likely expecting me. She's such a sweet soul. I hate disappointing her. She reminds me so much of my younger sister, Diana, back home in Hounddale."

"Your family doesn't live in Embervein?" I ask, unable to hide my surprise. I just assumed.

She shakes her head. "No. Only Alex and I live here. The rest of our family lives back in Hounddale. My father is a farmer, but Alex was never meant for farming. He's a soldier through and through."

"Alex?" I ask and she laughs.

"Ehren calls him Bram, so I suppose that's likely what you know him by, but he'll always be Alex to me."

I smile. "Ah. That makes sense. Well, may I accompany you to the library?"

She nods, giving me a warm smile. "I would like that very much."

"Why did you come to Embervein?" I ask as she leads the way. "I assume you have no interest in being a soldier for the prince."

She laughs again. Gods, I love that laugh.

"No, I came to visit my brother and to see Embervein. I saved up every possible marke so I could visit him. I was only supposed to stay a couple weeks before returning home, but both Alex and Ehren insisted I stay here until they can escort me back home personally. So, now I'm here."

I nod. "I suppose that's logical enough."

She turns her brown eyes to me. "Do you have any family in Embervein?"

I shake my head. "I don't have any family anywhere."

Her pink lips part slightly in surprise. "Oh, I'm so sorry."

I shrug. "I've been on my own for years now. It's not a bad life."

"It must be so very lonely," she says, her voice soft.

I turn my face to her, and she's staring at me with so much empathy it almost hurts. I force a smile.

"You get used to being alone. It's better that way sometimes."

She shakes her head, and I can tell she doesn't quite believe me.

"I would never want to be alone. I love people," she insists.

"Well, if I always had people around me like you, I would never want to be alone either," I offer and she blushes.

"Your accent," she says, tilting her head slightly. "I don't think I've heard one quite like it. Where are you from?"

I grin. "I spent most of my childhood in the Athiedor region."

"Oh! That's further north, correct?" I nod. "I've heard it's a beautiful area."

"It really is. I miss it," I confess.

We go around a corner, and I'm a little disappointed to discover that we've reached the library. She pauses, slipping her arm from mine.

"Well, I suppose this is goodbye for now, but I'll see you later, right?" She smiles softly, the smile reflected in her eyes.

"Most definitely."

Without thinking, I reach out and grab her hand. It's so small and pale against my own. I raise it to my lips and kiss her soft skin.

"Until we meet again," I murmur, heart racing.

"I will count the minutes."

She stands for a moment, looking deeply into my eyes, before she pulls her hand from mine, turning to enter the library. She pauses, halfway through the large oak door, glancing over her shoulder at me.

"I can't wait to get to know you more, Mr. Alak Dunne."

She offers me one last bright smile before disappearing. It takes me several moments to wake from what I'm sure must be a dream. For the first time in my life, I feel seen for me. I know Isabella knows next to nothing about me, nothing about my past, but everything about her—her smile, the way she looks at me, the way she treats me—makes me feel like she'll see past everything dark about me. That's a very new feeling and I rather like it.

Even as I wind my way back toward Ehren's room, I feel like I'm walking on air. I must convince Ehren and Bram to let me stay. I have to get to know Isabella. I can't imagine life without her, despite having met her mere minutes ago. When I finally find Ehren's room, I enter hesitantly. I have no idea what they decided while I was gone. Ehren's wide grin seems to indicate he won.

I eye Ehren cautiously and ask, "So, can I stay?"

"Of course!" Ehren declares.

Bram narrows his eyes. "But if you steal a single thing, you will find yourself out on the street again."

I throw my hands up defensively. "I'll be good, I swear."

I study Bram's face and decide that now is not the time to tell him I met his sister and am already madly in love with her.

"So, what do we do now?" I ask.

Ehren shrugs. "Do you play cards?" I nod. "All right, then how about we play cards until dinner?"

I nod, joining and Ehren and Bram at a table. Bram pulls out a deck of cards and we play. None of us are very good, so we don't bet money. We simply play and chat. It's fun and comfortable. Even Bram loosens up and is smiling before long. It probably helps that he wins most hands. When it's finally time for dinner, Bram collects his cards and I follow him and Ehren down to the dining hall. It's loud and filled with an energetic crowd. Ehren gives us a parting nod and makes his way to the head table, taking a seat next to a pretty, young girl about ten years old with long golden curls and bright blue eyes. Bram leads me over to a table consisting mostly of soldiers.

"Who's this?" a young soldier with dark eyes and hair asks, examining me closely.

"I'm Alak," I say, offering my hand.

The soldier raises his eyebrows in question but shakes my extended hand.

"You're no soldier," another one of the young men assesses. "You don't have the build for it."

"You're not wrong there," I chuckle.

"He is a friend of mine and Prince Ehren's," Bram says, clearing his throat as he takes a seat.

I smile and am about to take a seat next to Bram when I hear a delighted voice behind me.

"Oh! I was hoping to see you at dinner!"

I turn around and find Isabella standing directly behind me, eyes sparkling. Bram glares up with a frown.

"You two know each other?"

The others at the table exchange nervous glances. What have I stepped into here?

"Yes," Isabella says lightly, taking a seat next to her brother. "We met earlier in the stables. He has a lovely mare named Fawn." She looks up at me and gestures to the space on her other side. "Aren't you going to take a seat?"

Bram's cold glare settles on me as I sit down next to Isabella. I swallow and force a smile.

"Interesting. Alak forgot to mention that he met you," Bram says slowly. Somehow it sounds like a threat.

I try to act casual and shrug it off. "Did I? Sorry, mate. Busy day."

I suspect there's a lot more Bram has to say on the matter, but whether it's due to the fact that we're very much in public or the fact that dinner is starting, Bram closes his mouth in a tight line. I'm grateful for the distraction of food. I can't even remember the last time I ate a full meal. I shovel food in my mouth as fast as I can. I join in the conversation on occasion, but mostly I listen. Prince Ehren's escape from the carriage seems to be the main topic. The others try to pry details from Bram, but he only smiles and constantly changes the subject. I grin. Bram may be uptight, but he's loyal, I'll give him that. Every few minutes, Isabella looks over at me, and every time I forget how to form coherent sentences. By the end of dinner, I'm sure she thinks I'm an absolute idiot. When she rises, I stumble to my feet. She looks at me curiously.

"May I walk you to your room?" I blurt.

I feel the eyes of everyone else at the table boring into me, Bram's the strongest of them all. Isabella smiles, ignoring everyone else.

"I'd love that."

Bram shoots up from the table. "I will go with you."

Isabella rolls her eyes. "You're so overprotective."

I glance over at Bram. His face is set in lethal calm, one fist clenched at his side and the other gripping the hilt of his sword. I swallow and offer him a weak smile.

"Sure. Why not, mate?" I mutter. "The more the merrier."

Isabella sighs and glares at her brother. I follow her out of the dining hall. We aren't very far when Ehren's voice calls from behind us.

"Hey! Wait for me!"

I turn as Ehren runs up to us, grinning.

"So," Ehren says when he catches up. "What're we doing now? Oh. Hello, Isabella."

Ehren blushes slightly as Isabella inclines her head and says, "Hello, Ehren."

Shite. I have a prince for competition. That does not bode well for my chances.

"We were walking Isabella back to her room," Bram says stiffly.

"Already?" Ehren asks. "The night is still young!"

"Well, what do you suggest?" Isabella asks, her eyes bright.

Ehren shrugs and looks around for inspiration. "We

could . . . take a walk in one of the gardens. They're lovely this time of night."

A broad smile breaks out across Isabella's face, and she nods enthusiastically. "Oh, yes! I'd love that."

Ehren grins. "Excellent."

I can tell Ehren is about to offer Isabella his arm, but I quickly jump in and offer mine to her first. She glances at me in amusement but accepts my arm all the same. Ehren's face falls as his eyes narrow at me.

We stand in the corridor for a moment before Isabella finally asks, "Well, are we going to a garden or not?"

Ehren clears his throat. "Of course. Of course. Let's go."

He leads the way through the castle to what I expect is one of many palace gardens. This one is absolutely beautiful, and Isabella seems to love it. Her face glows, and she can't stop smiling. Ehren heads to the center of the garden and takes a seat on the ground directly in front of a large marble fountain. We all settle around him in the grass.

"So, why didn't you go to Gleador?" Isabella asks at length, picking a small flower and twirling it in her delicate fingers.

Ehren shrugs. "I don't know." He runs his hand through his hair. "Probably because I don't want to have anything to do with castle politics. I definitely don't want to be forced to marry Princess Elaine."

"You are the prince and heir to the throne," Bram points out. "It is going to happen sooner or later. You have responsibilities."

Ehren sighs and leans back against the fountain. "I don't want them."

"It does not matter if you want them. You have them,"

Bram states matter-of-factly. "You can only dodge them for so long."

"I know. Believe me, I know. But is it so wrong to want a normal life? To want to marry for love?" As he says it he glances briefly at Isabella, who blushes and focuses more intently on the flower she's holding.

"There is nothing wrong with that," Bram says. "But just because you want something doesn't mean you get it."

Ehren looks crestfallen. I don't know why I care. I shouldn't care. I've known him for less than a day. I avoid looking at him and glance down, plucking random blades of grass in front of me.

"Well, since you didn't go to Gleador, does that mean we get to have a birthday celebration after all?" Isabella says, breaking the building tension.

Ehren laughs. "Actually, my father made it very clear at dinner that I won't get a birthday celebration of any kind."

"Oh, that's not fair at all," Isabella pouts. "Birthdays aren't the same without any celebration."

"Eh, it's not that bad," I mutter without thinking. I glance up and all eyes are on me. Isabella's forehead is wrinkled with concern. "I mean, I haven't celebrated my birthday in years. I still keep getting older, though." I try to force a smile, but it doesn't seem to lighten the mood.

"What do you mean you haven't celebrated your birthday in years?" Isabella asks, her voice quiet.

I shrug. "Exactly that. My birthdays came and passed. No one knew but me." I shift uncomfortably. "It's no big deal. Really."

"When is your birthday?" Isabella asks.

"It was almost two weeks ago."

"Did you at least have a cake?" she presses.

"No. I'm not even sure if I ate that day." I realize after the fact what that probably sounded like to her. I try to backtrack. "It was a regular day." That didn't help.

Something about her expression looks heartbroken. I hate it. I don't like the thought that anything I've said or done has hurt her in any way. I glance away from her and even Ehren and Bram look disturbed by my words.

"It's getting late," I say standing. "Would anyone mind if I headed inside?"

They don't speak at first. They only stare at me. Finally, Ehren finds his voice.

"No, that's fine. We should all probably head inside."

Everyone rises and we slowly wend through the garden, no one speaking. Isabella leads us to her room first. When we get to her door she turns to me.

"It was nice meeting you, Alak. I sincerely hope we get to know each other better in the coming days," she says, smiling softly.

I smile. "I'd very much like that."

She gives a parting nod to Ehren and her brother before disappearing into her room. I sigh and stare at the closed door for a moment.

"You hurt my sister," Bram says in my ear, making me jump, "and I will kill you."

I swallow and turn to face Bram. "I have no intention of hurting your sister."

His eyes are cold and hard. "You better not."

Ehren clears his throat. "Well, let's stop hovering outside her door. I feel stalker-ish."

Bram nods, and we leave, making our way back to

Ehren's room. Bram stops a door early, heading into his own room, but I follow Ehren to his. When we get inside, Ehren gestures around.

"Sleep anywhere. Make yourself comfortable." He turns and heads to his bedroom. "I'll be right in here if you need anything, but please, don't need anything." He gives me a quick grin and wink before disappearing into his bedroom.

I look around the room and can't believe I'm actually sleeping here tonight. I settle down on the closest couch and prop my feet up. It's comfortable. Too comfortable. After shifting around for several minutes trying to find the best position, I end up on the floor with a blanket I've pulled from the back of the couch. It's easier to get comfortable on the floor. I fall asleep, thoughts of Isabella dancing in my head.

FOUR

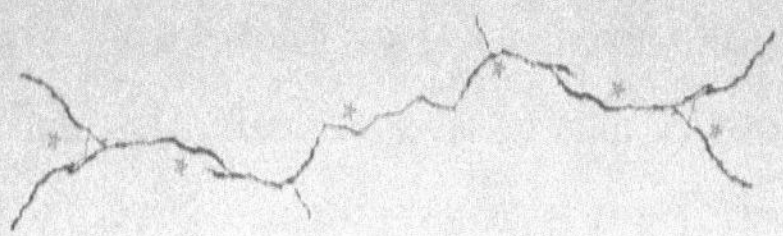

O h, you're still here."

I open my eyes to find Bram standing over me, arms crossed. I blink and sit up.

"Were you expecting me to abscond in the middle of the night with the royal jewels?"

"Actually, I was," Bram says. At first, I think he's serious, but there's a hint of a smile on his lips.

"Why are you on the floor?" Ehren asks, striding into the room dressed in a new outfit.

I shrug. "It was more comfortable?"

Bram studies me for a moment, then nods. "It took me awhile to get used to the beds here. They're too soft and comfortable. I imagine the couch is much the same."

"Too soft?" Ehren asks, arching an eyebrow. "How can a bed be too comfortable?"

Bram turns to Ehren while I stand. "When you're not used to it, it is an adjustment."

"I'll try again tonight," I promise, offering Ehren a smile.

Ehren shrugs. "Whatever suits you. I rang for breakfast, so someone should be up shortly with food."

No sooner has he spoken then there's a knock on the door.

"That must be breakfast now," Ehren says. "Come in!"

The door opens, but it's not a servant with breakfast. It's Isabella. She looks around the room until she spots me. A grin spreads across her face. I absentmindedly let my hand fly to my hair. I hope it's not sticking up everywhere.

"Good morning, Alak!" she says cheerily.

"Morning," I mumble, smiling.

Bram clears his throat. "What brings you by this morning?"

"I just had an idea I wanted to run by you and Ehren," she says, glowing. She's always glowing.

"But not me?" I tease.

She laughs. "Not yet."

Her eyes sparkle mischievously and my curiosity is piqued. She must detect my interest from my expression, and she laughs again. Beautiful, rich laughter.

"Don't worry," she assures me. "I'll tell you eventually."

"Well, what is it?" Ehren asks. "Please, tell me it's mischief. I need some more mischief in my life."

"Like hell you do," Bram grumbles. "Wasn't yesterday enough mischief for you?"

"Hardly!" Ehren replies, grinning wickedly.

"Well, I'll tell you, but I need to whisper it in your ear," Isabella replies, approaching Ehren.

Ehren's eyes widen, his lips parting as Isabella leans close to him. As her breath brushes his ear, he blushes. I can't help but feel a slight surge of jealousy that he gets to have Isabella so close to him. Whatever she says must be about me because Ehren's eyes dart my way more than once. When she pulls back, she's grinning.

"So," she presses. "What do you think?"

Ehren grins. "I like it."

Isabella claps her hands in delight. "Good! I hoped you would!"

"What is it?" Bram asks, scowling.

"I'll let Ehren fill you in!" Isabella says, brushing a quick kiss on her brother's cheek before walking toward the door. "I have a lot of things to do today." She glances toward me. "I'll see you later, Alak."

She holds my gaze for a moment longer than necessary before sweeping out of the room. When I pull my eyes away from the door, Bram's glaring at me.

"You hurt my sister . . ."

"I know. I know. You'll kill me."

"And I'll help," Ehren adds, voice uncharacteristically cold.

I'm saved by another knock at the door. This time it is breakfast. A servant enters with a tray bearing pastries and a pot of tea. I pick a pastry from the tray and pour myself a cup of tea while Ehren pulls Bram over to the side to fill him in on whatever Isabella said. When they join me, Bram is watching me closely. Whatever Isabella's plan entails definitely involves me.

"So," I say slowly. "What are the plans today?"

Ehren shrugs. "I'm supposed to still be on the road to Gleador, so I don't have any plans. Maybe we could—"

"No," Bram stops him.

"You don't even know what I was going to say!"

"I don't have to know what you were going to say in order to know it is not a good idea," Bram replies, crossing his arms.

Ehren rolls his eyes. "You really need to loosen up. I was going to suggest that we go and spar a bit in the sword ring."

Bram cocks his head. "Hmm. That is actually not a bad idea." He turns to me. "Are you any good with a sword?"

I nearly choke on my danish as I laugh. "Not in the slightest, mate. I'm not even sure I've ever held a sword."

Bram's eyes light up and he grins. "Well, I can show you exactly how good I am with a sword and all the ways I can kill you if you hurt my sister."

I go pale as Ehren laughs.

"Wow. You make it sound like such a fun day," I mumble. Ehren laughs harder.

"Come on," Ehren says, clapping his hand on my shoulder. "It could be fun. I promise, I won't let Bram murder you today."

"Fine," I concede.

After we stuff a few more pastries in our mouths and finish our tea, we head to what they call the upper training field. It's a wide, surprisingly flat section at the top of a hill surrounded by a short stone wall with a large stash of available weapons. For the first hour or so, I sit on the wall watching Ehren and Bram spar. It's clear that these two have fought together many times. They're both extremely talented, and I pity anyone who ends up on the other end of their swords. I make a note to never upset them. Ever.

After sparring for a while, they invite me to join them. I awkwardly select a sword from a nearby rack. It's heavy. Are all swords this heavy? I struggle to hold it up and Bram laughs. Ehren helps me select another sword. This one is a little lighter, but I still have no idea how to hold it, let alone fight with it.

Bram chuckles. "You are holding it all wrong."

I scowl. "I told you I have no idea what I'm doing. Not all of us were born on a battlefield."

"Here," Bram says, helping me adjust my grip. "Hold it like this." He stands back and assesses me before giving me a nod. "Much better. Now, stand like this."

I do my best to copy his stance. I feel incredibly awkward, but Bram nods again. Little by little he leads me in basic steps and movements. I'm hopeless. I don't understand half of what he's telling me, but I try to mimic his movements as best as I can.

"All right, now that you know the basics, let's spar," Bram suggests, grinning.

My eyes go wide, and I nearly drop my sword. "What?"

"I can go get the wooden swords the younger soldiers use," Ehren offers, grinning.

"Actually, can you?" I ask meekly. Bram and Ehren laugh.

"I will go easy on you," Bram promises.

I take a deep breath and assume the first stance Bram showed me. Bram lunges and, by some miracle, I manage to block him. I feel like I'm chaotically swinging my sword, but whatever I do seems to be overall effective because Bram doesn't manage to strike me for several blows. However, it doesn't take long for him to knock the sword from my hands. I stumble back, falling to the ground with a loud thump. He stands over me, grinning.

"Not bad. You actually have some potential. With a little work and some training, you could be decent."

"What?" I ask, brow furrowed in confusion. Was he really part of the same fight? I'm even more shocked when he offers me his hand. Hesitantly, I grab it and he hoists me to my feet.

"Maybe you aren't so bad after all," Bram says.

I just blink at him as Ehren laughs.

"Careful, Bram," Ehren says, slinging his arm across Bram's shoulders. "You're scaring the poor boy."

Bram rolls his eyes.

"While we're over by the training fields I'd like to go down and see how some of the soldiers are progressing," Ehren suggests, walking toward the gate.

"Still deciding the lineup for your perfect Guard?" Bram asks, falling into step beside Ehren.

Ehren grins. "Of course. You're still in line to be captain, you know."

"Your Guard?" I ask, a step behind.

Ehren nods. "Yep. Eventually, I get a Guard all my own. I'm going to fill it with the strongest and best soldiers. There're a few soldiers I already have my eye on. Some are already on my regular guard detail, but I need to make sure that my Guard is loyal to me first and foremost, rather than my father. That's also why I want soldiers from all over Callenia, not just Embervein."

"I am still not sure that is wise," Bram argues. "Without knowing them for several years, like you do most of the soldiers from Embervein, you cannot be sure of their loyalty."

"You're not from Embervein," I point out without thinking. Bram turns his sharp scowl to me.

"And how would you know that?"

"Isabella told me," I say with a shrug.

"How well, exactly, do you know my sister?" Bram asks, narrowing his eyes.

"Not terribly well. I just met her in the stables yesterday and walked her to the library. We chatted along the way. The only other times I've spoken to her were last night when you were present and then again this morning."

Bram considers my words and then nods. "Fine. Yes, you are correct. I did not grow up in Embervein, but I have trained side by side with Ehren for some time, so we know each other well. Other soldiers from outside Embervein won't likely have the same opportunity. I am a rare case."

"Still," Ehren cuts in, "there are many good soldiers just like you out there who deserve a spot on my Guard."

We stop at the edge of a training field, Ehren's eyes scanning the sparring soldiers. His gaze settles on one pair consisting of a tall, lean boy with dark skin and a shaved head sparring a shorter boy with dark brown hair and pale skin. It's obvious that the former is the more skilled of the two.

"Cal is coming along nicely in his training," Ehren muses with a pleased smile. "Any luck getting him moved to my guard detail yet?"

"You know your father doesn't listen to my opinion at all," Bram sighs. Disappointment flashes across Ehren's face, his smile faltering until Bram adds, "But I will keep trying."

"Cal will be the first invited to my Guard," Ehren says

firmly, the corner of his mouth twitching up into a small half-smile as he watches the soldier. "I know he's loyal and skilled."

Bram offers Ehren an assertive nod. "You couldn't ask for a better soldier."

Ehren continues observing the other soldiers, pacing along the edge of the field and mumbling to Bram occasionally. I get bored and begin placing bets in my head on which soldiers will win which fights. I'm actually quite good at assessing which are the most skilled soldiers, despite knowing little about sword fighting or fighting in general. Finally, after what seems like an eternity, we head back inside to eat lunch.

Halfway through lunch, a messenger informs Ehren he is wanted in a meeting. Ehren sighs dramatically before he and Bram head off into the belly of the castle. Without anything else to do, I join a few of the soldiers-in-training at a long table in the dining hall who are playing a game of dice. I watch for a while, learning the game, and eventually, they invite me to play a few rounds. No one is playing for money, which I appreciate since I have none. I completely lose track of time until they start clearing the tables to prepare for dinner. I wander out of the hall and find myself drifting toward the library. I stand outside the large carved doors, debating if I want to go inside and look for Isabella when I hear her voice from behind me.

"There you are!" she laughs. "I've been looking everywhere for you!"

I spin and face her, my cheeks turning red. "I, uh, I was looking for you, too."

"Apparently!" She looks at me, her eyes sparkling. "Come with me. I have a surprise!"

She extends her hand and I take it. It's so soft and warm. She smiles at me, pulling me along, heading in the direction of the gardens. The garden she leads me to is a different garden from last night, but it's equally beautiful. We wind through a maze of bushes to the center of the garden where I stop short. There's a long stone table with food scattered all down it. Behind the table stand Ehren and Bram, both grinning. The little princess from last night sits over to the side, her nose in a book.

"What's all this?" I ask, my eyebrows knit in confusion as I approach the table.

I look down at a simple yellow cake with five lit candles dripping wax. The words "Happy Birthday Alak" are scrawled in icing on top. I look up at Isabella, mouth gaping.

"What is this?" I ask again, quieter this time.

Isabella's eyes shine as she answers, "It's your birthday party! Sorry it's a couple weeks late."

"You made me a cake?"

Isabella's laugh is like sweet, rich honey. "Of course! Everyone should have cake for their birthday."

Ehren nods with emphatic agreement. "It's not a proper birthday without cake."

Tears well in my eyes. "I . . . I don't even know what to say."

"You don't have to say anything," Isabella insists. "Just enjoy!"

I look past Isabella to Ehren. "But isn't it *your* birthday?"

Ehren grins and shakes his head. "Not until tomorrow. Tonight's all about you."

I shake my head, fighting back tears.

"Hurry! Blow out your candles!" Isabella says. "Make a wish!"

I take a step closer, staring down at the flickering candles before looking back up at the others—my friends? They all watch me, smiling. Even Bram. I glance at Isabella. I don't need to wish for anything. Right now, I have more than I ever could wish for. I suppose that's my wish—that I can stay here forever with these people. Actually make friends. Be someone who's worth something. Someone people care about. I blow out the candles with a grin. Isabella claps her hands.

"Do you want to eat first or open presents?" she asks.

"Presents? What do you mean?" I ask, bewildered.

Isabella laughs. "It's your birthday party! We have presents!"

"Be forewarned," Ehren cuts in, grinning, "we only had a little heads up, so I'm afraid we don't have much."

I shake my head in disbelief. "I don't deserve any of this."

Bram offers me a small smile. "Birthdays are not about what you deserve. They are about celebrating your life." He hands me a small package wrapped in brown paper. "Happy birthday."

My hands are shaking as I unwrap the gift and find a small, simple dagger in a black sheath. I look up at Bram as I weigh it in my hand. "Thank you."

He shrugs, but his eyes glisten mischievously. "Maybe you will have better luck with a dagger than a sword."

I laugh. "Well, I can't imagine being much worse."

Ehren steps forward, handing me a lumpy package. I

unwrap it and find a pair of boots. They're brand new. I look up at Ehren wide-eyed.

"Boots?"

He nods. "They were made for me but I've never worn them. I have so many pairs. I noticed earlier that yours are a little worn."

I glance down at my feet. My boots are so worn they have holes. They're also a size too small. I kick them off, trying on the new pair. They fit perfectly. I stand and look over at Ehren.

"These are the nicest things I've ever owned. Thank you."

Ehren shrugs me off. Isabella clears her throat, drawing my attention. Her face is flushed pink.

"I didn't have a chance to really get you a present."

"You didn't have to. This whole thing is present enough." I smile softly at her and her flush deepens.

"Well, I still feel like you deserve something so . . ." She drops off and looks away for a moment before rushing at me and pressing her lips quickly to mine. It's brief, our lips barely touching long enough for me to even register the kiss, but it's enough to make my own cheeks flush a deep red. Bram makes a strangled choking sound but doesn't immediately try to murder me, which I greatly appreciate.

"Well, uh, that . . . Thank you," I mumble, glancing away and running my hand through my hair.

"You're welcome," she replies.

"So, cake?" Ehren cuts in awkwardly.

I turn back to the others and nod. "Yes, cake sounds excellent."

We pass the following hour laughing and eating. The

little princess in the corner barely looks up from her book, and I can't help but wonder how Isabella managed to get the girl to join us in the first place. Once she's had her piece of cake, she excuses herself and goes back inside. The rest of us stay outside until the moon is high above us. I'm sitting on the edge of the group, watching Isabella talking with her brother, when Ehren settles down next to me. He follows my gaze to Isabella.

"I think she really likes you," Ehren says quietly, sounding somewhat resigned.

I look up at him. "I feel like I should apologize."

Ehren chuckles. "I wish I could say I don't have any feelings for her, but, alas, I do. But she's never seemed to return them. I think she sees me as another brother." He sighs. "But you, she likes. I can see it."

Even as he says it, Isabella looks over at me and grins, her cheeks turning pink. I return her smile. She turns back to Bram, who is saying something to her, but she still watches me out of the corner of her eye.

"You're better for her, I think," Ehren says slowly.

I look at him in disbelief. "What? How? You're a prince. I'm . . . nothing. I'm less than nothing."

"That's just it, though. I'm a prince. If my father decides I need to marry Princess Elaine of Gleador then I'll marry her. I can't stand the thought of breaking Isabella's heart, so I'll never pursue a relationship with her, no matter my feelings. You don't have that problem. You can marry whomever you want." His eyes are watching Isabella with such an intense sadness, I feel for him.

"Maybe you'll get lucky and get to marry for love," I offer weakly.

He attempts a smile, but it doesn't go to his eyes. "Maybe, but I doubt it." He pauses and looks at me, his face shifting into an oddly intense expression. "Can I give you some advice, though, about Isabella?"

I nod and he takes a deep breath before continuing.

"Isabella has very high highs and very low lows."

I scowl. "What do you mean?"

"I mean," he says, searching for the right words, "she feels things more intensely than anyone I've ever known. When she's happy, she's on top of the world, but when she's sad . . ." His voice trails off and he shakes his head. "Just be careful with her."

I nod. "I will."

I rise and head back over to Bram and Isabella. Ehren follows suit.

"Did you enjoy your birthday celebration? Were you surprised?" Isabella asks as I approach.

I laugh. "Very surprised. This was easily one of the best days I've had in years."

"Really?" she asks breathlessly.

"Really."

Bram clears his throat pointedly, and I tear my gaze away from his sister and address him and Ehren. "Thank you all for helping. I really do appreciate it."

"All we did was show up," Ehren says, grinning. "Isabella was the mastermind."

Bram nods with a shrug. "It is true."

"Still," I insist. "You showed up and even brought gifts. I appreciate it. I really do. You have no idea what this means to me."

We all stand awkwardly for a moment before Ehren

shakes it off. "Well, I'll head on inside and send the servants out to clear the food, I think. Bram, come with me."

Bram eyes me and shakes his head. "I think I will stay out here a bit longer."

"Nope," Ehren says, "you're coming with me."

Ehren loops his arm around Bram's shoulders and drags him toward the castle.

"But . . . ," Bram protests, struggling out from Ehren's grasp.

"With. Me. Now."

With a sigh of frustrated resignation, Bram follows Ehren out of the garden, throwing me a dirty look before he disappears around the corner. I look over at Isabella, and her cheeks flush. She's such a nervous creature, and I can't help but love that about her. I offer her my arm.

"May I walk you to your room?"

She nods, taking my arm. We stroll through the garden at a leisurely pace, in no rush to be anywhere. She rests her head against me as we walk. My heart races, and I hope to the gods she can't hear it.

"I think your present was my favorite," I mutter, my voice rougher than I like.

She lifts her head and meets my eyes. "I enjoyed giving it to you."

We pause just outside the castle entrance, and she looks up at me. The golden flecks in her eyes look like stars in the moonlight. My breath catches as she slowly lifts her lips toward mine. Without hesitation I lean down and meet her halfway, pressing my lips to hers. This kiss is much more than the peck she offered me before. This is a real kiss. My first real kiss. When she finally pulls away, it's too soon. I lean back in and draw her against me, wrapping my arms around her. The kiss is eager, and she replies with her own eager kiss. This time when we pull back, we're both breathless.

She holds my gaze for a moment before whispering, "I think I'll see myself to my room, but I'll see you later, Alak."

I stand, frozen to the spot, my heart racing wildly as I watch her go. I'm so caught up in my thoughts I don't hear anyone come up behind me.

"Well, isn't that interesting," a voice drawls.

I spin and find Dylan, the boy from the tavern, standing behind me, a feral grin on his lips.

"What?" I bite.

Dylan raises his eyebrows. "Well, there's no need for that attitude."

"What did you find interesting?" I repeat, clenching my fists by my sides.

"Well," Dylan says, taking a step toward me, "I find it interesting that you've been here for barely a day, and you're already after Isabella. As if she would stoop so low to marry a street urchin like yourself." My eyes flash and he laughs. "Oh, yes, you can dress up in all the fancy clothes you want, but the fact remains that you're a nobody. Isabella won't want to marry a nobody."

"Feck off, mate," I snap. Dylan just laughs.

"Look, how about we make a little wager. You kiss Isabella like that again in front of her brother. If you get away with it, I'll give you ten markes."

My eyes go wide, betraying me. Ten markes is a lot for someone like me, and Dylan knows it.

"Isabella isn't something to bet on."

He shrugs. "Your loss. But you kiss her in front of her brother without getting decked or stabbed, and I'll give you ten markes." He shoves his hands in his pockets and begins sauntering off. "Think on it. Could be a great opportunity for you."

I'm still staring after him, seething, when the servants scuttle past me to go clean up what remains of our celebration. I shake my head and make my way back to Ehren's room. I want to forget everything Dylan said, but he made good points. I *am* a nobody. I may have Isabella's attention right now, but how long can that last? Ehren essentially gave me his blessing, but will Bram? It's really his opinion that matters.

When I get to Ehren's room I find it empty. Bram and Ehren must still be out doing important things. I settle down on the floor and fall asleep.

FIVE

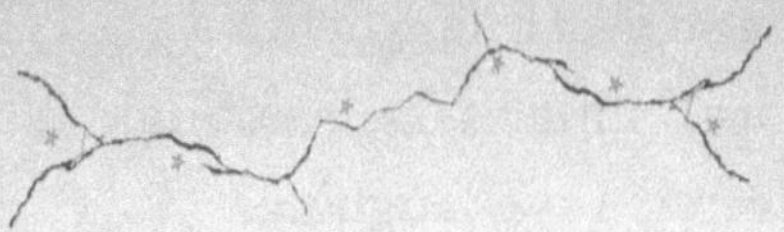

I'm awakened the next morning by Ehren yelling, "It's my birthday!" as loudly as he can. My reflexes kick in and I jump up from the floor. He chuckles.

"Sorry. I'm just excited to be fifteen."

"Happy birthday, mate." I grin. "What're your plans?"

He shrugs. "Honestly, I just want to stay out of the castle as much as possible. You know, avoid my father."

There's a knock on the door, and Bram enters without waiting for us to answer.

"I've had Mark and Peter prepare the horses," Bram says before Ehren can even say a word. He glances at me. "Yours is ready, too."

Ehren's eyes light up. "Really?"

Bram nods. "I figured you would want to get out of the castle as soon as possible. I also had Cook prepare some food for us to take, so we can stay out all day."

"I knew I kept you around for a reason." Ehren grins, throwing his arms around Bram.

"Yeah, yeah," Bram says, shaking Ehren off, but he doesn't bother trying to hide his smile. "Let's just get going, shall we?"

I follow Bram and Ehren to the stables and, sure enough, we find Solomon, Fawn, and a brown horse named Dauntless ready to go. We trot at a decent pace to the edge of town but pause at the edge of a long field.

"Want to race?" Ehren asks, eyes bright.

"Race to where?" I ask, laughing.

"Who cares? Let's just race!"

I laugh and we all take off, our horses galloping at full speed. I may not have been nearly as quick on foot as Bram and Ehren, but on Fawn, I'm the fastest. When we finally stop, Ehren and Bram eye Fawn.

"That is an excellent horse," Bram says as he dismounts.

"Thanks," I reply, hopping off Fawn. "My uncle got her for me when I was seven. She's been about the only constant in my life." I give her neck an affectionate rub.

"I have had Solomon since I was nine," Bram offers. "Nothing quite like the bond between a boy and his horse."

I nod in agreement. "So, what now?"

Ehren shrugs and plops down on the ground. "I'm happy just to lie in this field all day."

"That sounds like fun," Bram mutters under his breath.

"Well, what do you suggest?" Ehren challenges.

We all go back and forth for several minutes, but none of us can agree on anything. What we end up doing is a little bit of everything. We spar with swords, throw daggers, run, play cards, and dare each other to do all sorts of stupid things. After we eat our picnic lunch provided by Cook, we lie on our backs, staring up at the clouds.

"That one looks like a deer," Ehren muses.

"Which one?" I ask, tilting my head.

Ehren lifts his hand, pointing to the sky. "That one there, next to that big fluffy one that looks like ice cream."

"Oh, I see it."

"Your turn, Bram."

"This is stupid," Bram grumbles.

"Come on. It's my birthday," Ehren whines and Bram complies with a sigh.

"Fine. That one looks like a sheep."

I snort. "They all look like sheep. They're clouds. They're inherently sheep-like."

"Well this one looks more sheep-like than the others," Bram says sternly. Ehren and I break out in laughter. Bram scowls. "What? I am playing your stupid game! I see a sheep, damn it!"

His reaction makes Ehren and I laugh even harder. Bram tries to get us to stop, but, eventually, he gives in and laughs right along with us. We lie there laughing for several minutes. When we've finally settled down Ehren says, "I see one that looks like a cotton ball," and we're laughing again.

By the time we head back to the palace, the sun is close to setting. We've been out all day doing absolutely nothing, and it was wonderful. The only down point is that I didn't get to see Isabella.

When dawn breaks the next morning, my head is filled with thoughts of Isabella. Ehren has princely duties today that will keep him occupied, so I figure it might be a good day to get to know Isabella a little more. As soon as I'm dressed for the day, I rush to the library. I throw open the door and am immediately overwhelmed by how vast it is.

I'm staring up at the floors and floors of books when a small voice interrupts my thoughts.

"What're you doing in my library?"

I turn around to find the small, golden-haired princess scowling at me, her hand on her hip.

"Oh, hello there, love. I'm looking for Isabella. Is she here?"

The princess lets out a long, exasperated sigh. "She's not here yet. She's probably still in her room."

And with that, the little girl turns and bounces away, ignoring me entirely. With a shrug, I leave the library and head toward Isabella's room. When I get to her door I freeze. Do I have the right room? Is she in there alone? What will she think about me just showing up? I'm running an inner monologue, about to talk myself out of knocking when the door opens. Isabella nearly crashes into me and takes a step back, blinking.

"Alak? What are you doing here?" she asks, staring at me wide-eyed and curious.

"I, uh, I wanted to see if you, uh, wanted to spend the day with me?" I fumble, playing with the edge of my shirt.

Isabella grins. "I'd love to! I just need to go to the library for a bit, but I can meet you in an hour. Would that work?"

Relief washes over me and I grin. "Aye, that'll be perfect. I'll meet you in front of the stables in an hour."

"Sounds good." She pauses and then asks, "Will you walk me to the library?"

I offer her my arm. "It would be my pleasure."

Once Isabella is safely deposited at the library, I rush off to make more plans for the day. First, I find the kitchens. I locate the woman everyone calls "Cook" and ask her to help me prepare a picnic.

"And who's this girl you're trying impress?" she huffs, going about her work, not even bothering to look at me.

"Um, Miss Isabella Bramfield. I don't know if you know who she is . . ."

"I know her. She's sweet." Cook pauses, her eyes narrowing as she studies me. "Fine. Come back in a few minutes and I'll have something ready for you. Now, out of my kitchen!"

Next, I wander into the city itself. I want to get Isabella a gift. I have a few coins that I managed to steal my first day, but it's not much. I can't find anything worthy of Isabella in my price range. I turn from vendor after vendor, my face crestfallen. Maybe I should take Dylan up on his stupid bet. Then I could have ten markes to buy her a decent gift. With a sigh, I resign myself to picking a few wildflowers growing on the side of the road. I grab my packed lunch from Cook and head to the stables to wait.

I anxiously pace outside the stables, watching the path from the palace like a hawk. When Isabella finally appears, my heart starts racing. I half expected her not to show up. When she reaches me, I thrust the flowers I picked toward her.

"I wanted something as lovely as you." It's a stupid line, but it makes her smile.

"I love them!"

"Would you like to go for a ride? I thought maybe we could go into the woods. There's a little river that we could go see, and then we could have a picnic."

Her eyes light up. "A picnic?"

I nod, holding up the basket from Cook.

"That sounds lovely."

"All right. Well, I have Fawn, but we'll need to get you a horse."

"Do you think . . . I mean, would you mind if I rode with you on Fawn?" She looks up at me through her long eyelashes, and I suddenly find it nearly impossible to breathe. She takes my silence as a no and quickly begins to backtrack. "I mean, if you don't want to that's fine. I understand."

"No, I definitely want that. It's fine." I swallow hard and her smile returns, brighter than before.

I extend my hand and she takes it, linking her fingers with mine. I lead her inside the stables and Mark, Peter's older brother, greets us. A few minutes later, I help Isabella up on Fawn and climb up behind her. Her hair smells like roses, and it's the most beautiful smell in the whole world. I wrap my arms around her, and she leans back against me as we ride. I could die happy right now, and if Bram saw me, he would probably be happy to kill me. But I don't care.

I lead Fawn out of the city and into the trees. On horseback it doesn't take long to find the water. I dismount and offer my hand to Isabella. She takes it with a smile and drops into my arms. We stay frozen like that for a minute before I release her and jerk back, running my hand through my hair. She giggles.

"What now?" she asks, walking toward the river. "It's still too early for lunch. Should we swim?" She glances at me over her shoulder.

My thoughts start to go wild. Honestly, I would love to see Isabella stripped down to practically nothing, all wet. I drive the thoughts from my mind. Bram *would* kill me. Swimming would also mean me stripping down, and I'm not ready for Isabella to see my scars. I shake my head.

"I don't want to swim, but we could maybe wade a little?"

She nods eagerly and sits down on the ground, removing her shoes. I do the same, kicking off my new boots. Isabella lifts up the hem of her dress and dips a tentative toe in the water.

"It's cold," she gasps.

"Is it?" I ask, approaching the water. When I get close she splashes me with water.

I inhale sharply.

"Sorry," she says, covering her mouth as she giggles. "I couldn't resist!"

I laugh and splash her in turn. For several minutes we laugh and splash each other until we're both soaked. Isabella wades further out into the water and takes a seat in the stream, the flowing water splashing over her lap.

"What are you doing?" I ask, cocking my head.

"Well," she replies. "I'm soaked anyway. Might as well enjoy the water. Want to join me?"

I hesitate and then slowly wade into the freezing water, taking a seat by her side. She leans over, resting her head against me, and I wrap my arm around her. She's so perfect. I don't deserve her.

"Isabella," I say, slowly. "I think . . . I think I may love you."

She pulls away from me and looks up into my eyes, her own eyes wide. "What?"

I shake my head, embarrassment coloring my cheeks. "Never mind. Nothing."

"No," she says, reaching a hand up and gently touching my cheek. "No, say it again."

I look into her gold-speckled eyes. "I—I love you."

A smile spreads across her lips as she takes a deep breath. "I love you, too, Alak."

Her words stop my heart.

"I know it may seem silly," she continues, "and I know we're still young, and we haven't known each other all that long, but I know my heart. I've never felt about anyone the way I feel about you. This has to be love, right?"

I nod. "I think it must be."

I slowly lower my lips to hers, and she accepts my kiss eagerly. When I pull back there are tears in her eyes.

"What's wrong?" I ask, concern flooding my voice as I furrow my brow.

She shakes her head. "I'm just so happy."

I pull her tighter against my body and she snuggles into me.

"I know we're young yet, but do you think you'd ever be willing to marry me?" Isabella asks at length.

My shoulders sink.

"Isabella . . . ," I start, not knowing how to find the words. Worry and hurt flash on her face. "I want to. I really do. One day. But I'm nobody. I have nothing."

"I don't need anything besides you," she says softly.

I smile weakly. "That's not enough to live, and I can't ask

that of you. I can try to find a job. Get some money. Then maybe we can make it work."

She smiles. "I can wait. I'll wait a lifetime for you, Alak."

Her voice is so sincere. I want to make this work. I want to be the person she thinks I can be. In three years, I'll be eighteen. Many people get married then. Surely, in three years' time, I can make something of myself.

"Are you okay?"

I realize I've been wrapped up in my thoughts for several minutes. I smile. "I'm fine. I'm just planning a future with you in it."

She releases a happy sigh, and I kiss the top of her head. She shifts and looks toward the shore.

"You brought lunch, right? I think I could eat now."

I laugh and stand, offering her my hand. She takes it and we splash to the shore. Cook provided us with a decent lunch of cold ham, cheese, and bread. We sit quietly and eat for a while, just enjoying being together. When we're done, we pack up everything and head back to the castle, even though we're both still soaking wet. Bram leans against the edge of the stable doorway, staring us down as we approach. I swallow. When we reach the stables, I dismount Fawn just outside and help Isabella down.

"Did you have a good day?" Bram asks, his voice flat.

"It was the best day," Isabella says breathlessly.

Bram scowls, but I grin, my heart fluttering in my chest.

I mumble something about taking Fawn inside and leave Bram and Isabella to talk alone for a few minutes. When I come back outside, Isabella and Bram seem to be deep in conversation. I hang back and glance around the courtyard. My heart drops when I see Dylan not too far away, leering at me. When he realizes I'm looking at him, he waggles his eyebrows and puckers his lips, kissing the air. I shake my head ever so slightly, and he shrugs, holding up a small coin pouch. I try to ignore him, walking over to Isabella. Bram eyes me steadily.

"Isabella was telling me about your day. It seems you had a lot of fun," he says stiffly.

I nod and smile. "We had an excellent day."

I look past Bram to find Dylan still watching us. I clench my fists at my sides. I'm little more than entertainment to him, but I really could use those coins. Before I can talk myself out of it, I reach over and pull Isabella into a kiss. She's surprised at first, but quickly returns the kiss. When I pull back I almost forget about Bram standing there until he speaks.

"What exactly are you doing with my sister?" he snaps, clenching both hands into fists at his sides, eyes flashing with pure fury. I stumble back a little.

"Sorry, I—" I start but Isabella cuts in.

"I love him, Alex," she says jutting her chin out defiantly as she slides her hand into mine. "And he loves me."

Bram's eyes lock with mine and I can feel his anger. He doesn't like me much at the moment, and I can't blame him. Another look at the pure innocence shining on Isabella's face and he relaxes. He inhales, slowly releasing a long breath.

"Fine. Just . . . be careful. Let's go inside, shall we?"

Bram turns and leads the way into the castle. Heart pounding, I follow him, Isabella's hand still in mine. We're nearly to the stairs when Dylan bumps into me.

"Oh, sorry," he mumbles as he shoves something into my hand, eyes gleaming.

He stumbles away, and I tighten my hand around the coin pouch he slipped me. Without drawing any attention to the pouch, I slide it into my pocket. Isabella can never know about this. No one can ever know about this.

SIX

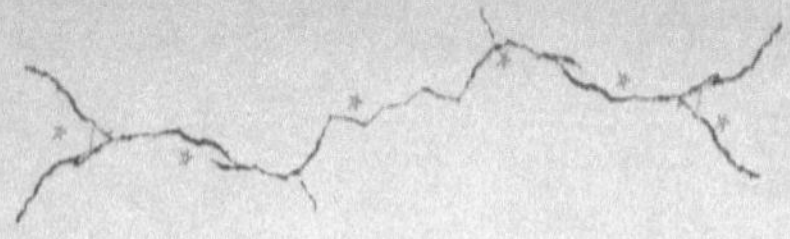

I sleep restlessly. Every time I close my eyes, I see Dylan's face mocking me.

"You'll never be good enough for her," he sneers. "You can never make money on your own. You can only succeed with me."

And then his face fades into my father's, and he's yelling at me. I'm ten years old again, cowering in fear.

"You're worthless, boy!" he spits. "Why would anyone want you?"

He starts hitting me, and I lie there, trying to keep him from damaging my face. I cry. They're both right. I'm worthless, and no one—especially not Isabella—would want me.

I wake with a gasp to find Ehren over me, his face etched with concern.

"Good. You're awake. Are you okay?" Ehren asks, eyes scanning my face.

I sit up, shaking my head to clear it as I rub the sleep from my eyes. "Aye, mate," I mutter. "I'm fine."

Ehren breathes a sigh of relief and leans against the couch. "You were mumbling in your sleep and seemed distressed."

"I think I was having a nightmare."

Ehren nods knowingly and rises. "Well, if you're sure you're okay, I have to be somewhere. There's breakfast over on the table if you're hungry."

I nod. Ehren starts to walk toward the door, but I stop him.

"Hey, you don't happen to know anywhere I could get a job, do you?"

Ehren grins. "You tired of sleeping on my floor already?"

I force a smile. "I was just thinking that if I'm going to stick around for a while, I might as well try to find a job, and, you know, make some sort of living."

"Well," Ehren muses, "I have to confess that I don't really keep up with that sort of thing. I kind of have my entire life planned out for me."

"Oh, yeah. I suppose that's true."

"I'm sure you could find something in the city. People are always looking for others to work for them, I suspect."

I sigh, absentmindedly raking my hand through my hair.

"I wish I could be more help, but you're welcome to stay here as long as you need to. I won't kick you out."

My smile is more genuine this time. "Thanks, Ehren. I really appreciate it."

He offers me one last smile before rushing off to do whatever is demanded of him today. I explore the castle a bit before finally heading into town. I stop at almost every vendor and business, but no one is looking for workers.

Finally, I stumble into the tavern. The man narrows his eyes at me.

"You're that troublemaker from a few days back," the man grunts.

I force my face into the most innocent look I can. "Please, sir, I was just wondering if you had any work available."

"Work, eh?" he asks, not looking quite convinced I'm not up to something far more devious. "What sort of work are you willing to do?"

"Anything, really."

He studies me for a moment and finally says, "I actually do need someone to help clean up during the day. You'd be responsible for keeping the tables clean, and the floors, and washing the dishes, and even cleaning the rooms upstairs when needed."

None of that sounds pleasant, but it doesn't sound too bad either. I nod. "I can do all that. When should I start?"

The man's eyes shift to a massive stack of dirty mugs and plates behind him. "You can start now if you want. Come in every day first thing and clean up from the night before, and I'll pay you at the end of each day."

I nod eagerly and set to work. I expect the job to be easier than it is. Most of these plates and mugs are completely crusted in layers of food that do not want to come off. I'm hours into the day and not even nearly done. Of course, it doesn't help that there's a constant flow of patrons adding more and more to my pile. The busier it gets, the more often I have to stop washing the dishes to clean up messes on tables and the floor. The highlight of my day is cleaning up puke. That happens three times. It's gross and disgusting. When the dinner rush starts, two others show up to take my place. One is a busty girl, who's there mostly to wait tables, and the other a boy younger than I am, who takes over most of my work. I'm exhausted and surprisingly sore as I go to leave.

"Wait a minute, boy," the barkeep calls after me. I turn back to him with a glazed expression. He laughs and holds out his hand. "Your pay."

I extend my hand eagerly, but my face falls when he drops two coins in my hand—one marke and a half-marke. It's not much for a full day of work, but I shouldn't have really expected more for my first day. He notices my disappointment.

"The longer you work for me, the more I'll give you. Just keep coming back, boy."

I nod and shove the coins in my pocket. The walk back to the palace seems to take forever. I've been standing most of the day, and my legs and back are aching. I've already started to get blisters on my hands. All for two lousy coins. I'm debating if all that work was worth it when I hear my name called across the castle courtyard.

"Alak! There you are!" Isabella cries, rushing toward me. Her face is a bright light at the end of a dark day. I smile.

"Were you looking for me, love?" I ask, grinning through my exhaustion.

She nods. "All day! Where have you been?"

"I got a job at The Gilded Goblet."

"A job? Why?" Her confused expression is exceptionally endearing.

"Well, the way I see it, if I'm going to save up enough money to buy you gifts and all the things you deserve, I need to make some honest money," I say and her expression softens.

"Oh, Alak," she whispers. "I don't need anything from you."

She reaches out and places her hand on my cheek. I lean into her gentle touch and she smiles.

"Really, Alak, you're enough for me the way you are."

My heart skips a beat. If only everyone could see me the way Isabella does. Without any hesitation, I reach out and draw her closer, pressing my lips to hers. When we pull apart, her eyes are shining. I look down at her and brush a stray hair from her face.

"I love you, Isabella, and, while you may not demand the world, I want to give it to you. You deserve the world. What kind of person would I be if I didn't at least try to give it to you?"

She smiles and lifts her lips to mine again. I'm lost in her kiss. Time has no meaning. No one else in the world matters right now beyond Isabella. I could easily stay like this forever, my arms wrapped around her, her lips pressed to mine, but eventually, we break apart. I slide my arm around her waist as we make our way back inside.

It's late in the evening, but dinner is still going on. We join Bram and others at a table and eat what we can. I'm so exhausted from my day, I don't join in most conversations. If anyone notices I'm quieter than usual, they don't say anything. After dinner, Isabella and I take a quick walk in a garden. The stars sparkle like diamonds above us. It's perfect. She's perfect. By the time I finally leave her at her room and head to Ehren's, I'm practically sleepwalking.

"You look dead on your feet," Ehren observes when I stumble through the door. "I assume you found a job?"

I nod. "Yeah, at the tavern."

Ehren's eyes light up with delighted mischief. "That sounds like an *excellent* job."

I laugh. "I don't actually serve any of the drinks, so I can't help you out, mate. I'm just cleaning up."

"Oh, well then," Ehren replies, his face falling a bit. "But it's good you found a job. I'm happy for you. Remember, you're always welcome here."

I nod, truly grateful. "Right now I just want to sleep."

"Well, I'll let you be," Ehren says, striding to his door. "I'll see you in the morning."

I see very little of Ehren, or anyone else, the next several days. I'm up at dawn heading down to the tavern before most of them have woken. The earlier I get to work, the sooner I'm done. I have blisters on my hands, all my clothes smell like ale and puke, and I'm constantly tired. Every day I want to give up, but then I see Isabella and remember that this will all be worth it.

One day, I'm nearing the end of my shift when Dylan comes in with two of his friends. I should have been paying closer attention so I could avoid them. But I'm not, and he sneaks up on me.

"Well, well, well, what do we have here?" he grins, peering across the bar at me as I scrub a plate clean. "It looks like the street urchin is tired of riding the coattails of the prince! Or maybe, the prince kicked you out to find your own little hole?"

I glare at him. "Go away, Dylan."

Mock hurt flashes on his face. "Now, is that any way to talk to your benefactor?"

"Benefactor? Hardly," I huff. "You gave me ten markes on a lame bet."

"Oh, don't play coy. We both know that ten markes is a lot for you. Probably more than you've made working here in total, isn't it?"

I glance away, purposefully avoiding his eyes. He claps his hands in glee.

"I'm right! You make a pathetic pittance here. I must say, it's disappointing. Someone as ballsy as you deserves better. I mean, kissing Bramfield's sister like that right in front of him . . ." Dylan lets out a low whistle. I shake my head and turn away.

"I care for Isabella. Your bet had nothing to do with that kiss," I mumble, wishing to the gods my words were true.

Dylan laughs gleefully. "Whatever you need to tell yourself. But, if you do truly care for the girl, I think you'll find my next wager most enticing."

I look up at him and find him grinning like a feral cat. Behind him, his two friends are locked in interest on our conversation. I shake my head.

"I want nothing to do with your wagers, Dylan. I love Isabella. She's not a betting chip," I say, working hard to keep my voice steady.

"Not even for, let's say, fifty markes?"

I can't keep my shock from showing. Fifty markes could go a long way. I could quit this stupid job and find another one. I could buy Isabella a decent present and save the rest. I could actually have the beginnings of a future. I could be worthy of her.

"What would I have to do?" I ask slowly. Pure delight flashes on Dylan's face.

"All you have to do is have sex with her."

My face blanches as Dylan and his friends howl with delight.

"Come now, you can't tell me you haven't already thought about it. Isabella has amazing curves. Even I would be happy to see her splayed out, naked on a bed beneath my own body—"

"Shut up," I hiss, cutting him off as my face turns red. Dylan and his friends laugh while I try to push the image from my mind. "Isabella's a decent girl. She doesn't deserve to be treated that way."

"I'll add another fifty markes to the wager," one of Dylan's friends adds, grinning.

"Oh, now that's something!" Dylan says, eyes wide. "Jaiden never likes to part with his money. Tell me, street urchin, what could you do with one hundred markes?"

I consider the boys for a moment. One hundred markes is a life-changing amount. And Dylan isn't entirely wrong. I have thought about Isabella that way. Some nights kisses don't quite cut it. I do want more. I want her in every possible way.

"How would you even know if I slept with Isabella?" I ask. "My word? Because I'm sure as hell not going to do something like that in the courtyard in front of her brother."

Dylan laughs. "Naturally, I would assume you would do it behind closed doors. But I'll know. Trust me."

"Fine, I'll think about it," I mutter.

Dylan and his friends grin, amused by my pain.

"For once," Dylan says with an evil grin, "I'm hoping I

actually have to pay this wager, if only to watch you squirm."

He and his friends cackle as they finally leave me be and head to a table to drink until they're completely pissed. I get back to work. I want more than anything to leave and get away from them. I hate them with every fiber of my being. When I'm done for the day, I go to get my daily pay.

"I heard a bit those boys were saying to you earlier," the barkeep says as he hands me my coins. "You're working here for a girl?"

I nod wearily, too tired and frustrated to speak.

"We've all been there, boy," he replies, sympathetically. "And first love is always the hardest. I assume this girl is your first love?"

I nod again.

"Well, boy, maybe she'll be your last love, maybe not. But don't let her define you and make all your decisions. You're a good, hard worker. You have potential in this world."

I look up at him. "Isabella is the only love I'll ever have in my life. I don't want or need anyone else."

He nods with a half-shrug. "Maybe you're one of the lucky ones who really did find your one true love early in life. Maybe you'll never have your heart broken. But if you do, just remember there may be someone else out there for you."

"And what do you know about love?" I scoff, glancing away.

He considers me for a moment before answering. "I've been married twice. Lost both in childbirth many years ago."

I look back up at him. "I'm sorry."

"It's all right. I wouldn't trade the love I felt for either of them for anything in this world." He pauses before adding, "Now, get on out of here. I'll see you in the morning."

I nod and leave, slipping the coins in my pocket. I'm physically and mentally drained. I know I love Isabella. She's the only love I need. She's the only love I want. And if I love her, if I truly love her, which I do, what's so wrong about sleeping with her? I can fulfill my needs and desires and make some money. It's a winning situation all around.

When I get to the castle, I don't even bother going to the dining hall. Tonight, hunger isn't first and foremost on my mind. Instead, I go straight to Ehren's room and wash up. I change my clothes and tie back my hair. I pace back and forth in his sitting room for at least an hour. I keep expecting Ehren and Bram to come in and mess up my plans. I halfway want them to. I want someone to come and talk some sense into me. I want someone to stop me. The fact that I'm even considering Dylan's ridiculous offer shows how pathetic and desperate I am. But, I tell myself, I won't do anything Isabella doesn't want to do. If she accepts my offer—if she *wants* to have sex with me—then there's nothing wrong with it. Right?

Finally, I'm done with wavering. Before I can talk myself out of it, I march from Ehren's room to Isabella's. I knock on her door with far more bravado than I feel. When she opens the door, she's wearing nothing but a simple, thin night dress. My breath catches and her eyes go wide.

"Alak? What are you doing here? I didn't think I would get to see you today," she says, her eyes bright.

I laugh nervously. "Are you upset to see me, love?"

She shakes her head. "No. I'm always happy to see you."

Footsteps echo nearby, so I glance around before asking, "Would it be all right if I came in?"

Her lips part and I'm sure she's going to turn me away, but she nods slowly, opening her door a little more. I take a deep breath and exhale it slowly as I slide past her into her room. It's a smaller, more feminine version of Ehren's. She closes the door and turns to me, her hands clasped in front of her.

"Alak," she asks, slowly, unsure. "Why are you here?"

Her eyes find mine, and I suspect she knows exactly why I'm here. She doesn't know about the bet, I'm sure, but she *knows*. Why else would I push into her room this time of night? Why else would I invite myself in when she's clearly ready for bed?

"Isabella . . ." I stare at her unable, to form words.

She smiles softly and walks up to me. For moment she holds my gaze and then lifts her lips to mine. The kiss starts out simple but quickly turns into much more. There's heat and longing. My hands search her body, and hers mine. She pulls back with a pleased gasp.

"Do you . . . do you want to go into the bedroom?" she asks, her voice low and sultry.

I swallow. "Very much."

She takes me by the hand, leading me into her bedroom. She drops her nightdress and stands completely exposed and naked before me. Her body is like porcelain, pure and beautiful. I discard my own shirt, heedless of my scars, and quickly cover the small space between us. She lies down on the bed, and I take my place above her. I love the feel of her skin against mine. She loosens my pants and starts to slide them off. Oh, gods. It's really happening. My heart thrums in my chest, beating a fast, unsteady rhythm. I look down into her eyes. I can see her own longing there, a match to mine. I get to have her, and I'll get one hundred markes.

I jerk up and turn away from her, taking a seat on the edge of her bed. No. I can't do this while there's money on the table. I have to go back to Dylan and call off the wager. I have to know that this is right for me. I'm not ready for this. Not now. Not like this. It's not fair to Isabella. If we do this now, I'll always wonder if it was the money or if it was truly for love.

"Alak?" she asks, hesitantly, placing her hand on my shoulder. "Are you okay?"

I shake my head and drop my face into my hands. "I can't do this, Isabella."

I rise from the bed, pulling my pants up and grabbing my shirt. I walk away, but she calls after me.

"Wait! Alak, wait!"

I ignore her and rush from her bedroom, toward the door. I have to get out while I have my resolve. She runs after me. I throw open the door and stalk out into the hall, still shirtless. I don't expect her to run after me. She's undressed, but she's foolishly in love and not thinking clearly. She plunges into the hall, clutching her nightdress in front of her still naked body.

"Alak, what did I do wrong?" she pleads, her voice broken.

I spin to face her. My guilt swells around me like a storm.

"Get back inside!" I yell at her, my fury at my own stupid actions ringing in my words.

She's trembling, tears streaming down her cheeks. She's

broken and her brokenness breaks me. I did this. I broke a perfect thing. I don't know what to do. I don't know how to fix this. I don't . . .

"Please, Alak. Tell me what I did wrong," she begs. "Please."

Someone comes around the corner. A servant. I shake my head and rush off. I can't talk to her now. Shame fills me as I run from her. I have to put distance between us. How do I explain to her that she's done nothing wrong? How do I explain my own stupidity? How can I fix this? I just need time to think.

I wander the palace grounds for quite some time before I finally make my way back to Ehren's quarters. I don't want to face him. I can't face him. Thankfully, when I arrive he's already in his bedroom, door closed. I crash on the couch and fall into a restless sleep.

SEVEN

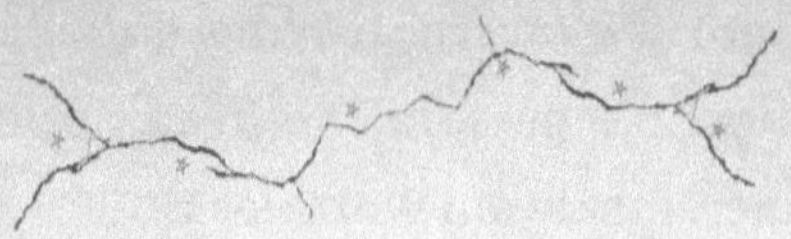

The next morning I rise a little later than usual. I hear Ehren wake, and I pretend to still be asleep until I'm sure he's gone. Even after he leaves, I lie there for several minutes before I find the motivation to get up. But, finally, I rise and head to the tavern for a day of work and drudgery. I figure by this time of the morning Isabella should already be in the library. I don't want to see her yet. I manage to make it out of the castle without seeing her, Ehren, or Bram, but I stop cold when I see Isabella waiting outside the tavern. She smiles softly as I approach. I avoid her gaze and try to shove past her, but she grabs my arm.

"Talk to me, Alak," she says, her voice breaking. "Please."

"I have nothing to say to you," I mumble. "I need to get to work."

I jerk from her grasp. One quick look at her face tells me she's in pain. Part of me wants to fix it. I want to hold her. I want to tell her it's not her fault. I want to make this better.

But I don't know how. A tear slides down her cheek, shattering my heart.

"Isabella," I start slowly, unsure. "I . . ." What can I say?

She looks at me expectantly. "Yes?"

I sigh, glancing away. "I told you I wasn't worth anything. You're better off without me."

I stumble into the tavern, leaving Isabella crying in the streets. I'm a horrible person. I've lived up to the expectations of my father. I truly am worthless.

I'm scolded for being late, as expected, but I don't care. I get to work right away, scrubbing and cleaning. It's nice to have the distraction from Isabella. I can't think about her. I know I've broken her heart. I hope she's not hurting as much as I am. Is there any way to fix this? I have to get Dylan to call off his wager. Then I can go to Isabella and give her what we both want. That can fix this. That's my best option.

I'm wondering how I can find and contact Dylan when he and his friends come in, laughing. When Dylan sees me, his eyes light up.

"Well, who knew you actually had it in you?" he asks, wicked glee dripping from his voice.

I shake my head. "I don't know what you're talking about."

"Don't you? I heard all about you and Isabella." He leans in and whispers, "If you don't want to be caught fleeing a girl's room after the deed, it's always best to wait until much later at night."

I take a shuddering breath. If he knows, who else knows?

"It's not what you think."

He laughs. "Isn't it though? But I'm a man of my word." He drops a coin pouch on the counter between us with a clank. "Here's my fifty markes. I'll get the rest from Jaiden later."

I glance at the bag and shake my head. "I don't want yer money." Sometimes I hate my stupid accent. It always gets thicker when I'm mad, betraying me.

"Don't be stupid. Take the money," Dylan insists, nudging the bag closer. "After all, you earned it. You got sex and money. Your life is pretty damn good right now."

I'm seething. I turn away from him and focus on cleaning a mug.

"Hey, take the damn money," he hisses. He's angry now. Good. That makes two of us.

"I don't want it," I growl, refusing to turn around.

"Take it."

I spin and face him. The laughter is gone from his face, replaced by fury and frustration. He's not used to being told no. I grin, finding strength in that fact.

"No."

He reaches across the counter and grabs my shirt in his fists, yanking me hard into the countertop. "You no good little . . ."

"Hey! Not in my bar!"

We look down the bar to see the barkeep glaring at us.

Dylan releases me with a jerk. "Fine." He turns and looks at me. "Take the money or not. It doesn't matter because you're still not worth a thing. How a boy like you got the interest of a girl like her in the first place, I'll never know."

He turns and stalks away with his friends. I release a long breath and turn back to my work. I can feel the eyes of the barkeep on me, but I don't look up. And I don't take the money.

When my workday finally ends, I slowly head back to the castle, but I don't go inside. I can't stand the thought of seeing Isabella. I still don't know what to say. I still don't know how to fix this. I head into the stables and find Fawn. She snorts happily when she sees me. I enter her stall and press my forehead to hers.

"What have I done, Fawn?" I murmur. I sigh and pull back, rubbing Fawn's neck. "Why are you the only girl I can take care of properly? Why are you my only friend?"

Fawn gives a snort and paws at the ground.

"I know I need to talk to her, but I don't know how. I don't know what to say. The thought of losing her forever is too painful. What if she hates me after I explain? What if she can't forgive me?"

I sink down in the corner of the stall, my head in my hands. "I've failed at life. Again."

I don't mean to stay in the stall all night, but at some point I drift off. I dream of Isabella over and over again. Her face covered in tears flashes in my mind on repeat.

"Why, Alak? What have I done?" her voice echoes over and over.

When I wake, my cheeks are wet with tears. I need to fix things with Isabella, now. I rise and leave the stables. It's barely dawn, so she should still be in her room. I rush through the castle, not paying attention to anyone or anything. My sole purpose is finding Isabella and fixing things. When I get to her door, I take a deep, steadying breath and knock. No one answers.

"Isabella?" I call, knocking again. "It's Alak."

I wait, but there's nothing but silence. Maybe she's already gone to the library. I knock again but there's still no answer. I'm about to turn and leave when I decide to go in her room. Maybe she's just on the other side of the door. Maybe she's avoiding me like I did her. I open the door and enter. Something is off. Something is wrong. But I can't place what, and that bothers me.

"Isabella?" I call out, closing the door behind me with a quiet click. "Are you here?"

A strange unease fills me as I approach her bedroom. The door is open. I can see a figure on her bed, lying there in the dark. I sigh with relief. She must still be sleeping. I smile softly and step toward her room. Then it hits me—the strong metallic scent of blood. My heart stops.

"Isabella?" I say, my voice shaking.

My whole body trembles as I approach the bed. I freeze a few feet away, staring in horror at the scene I've found. Isabella lies in the center of her bed completely still. Her gold-speckled brown eyes closed forever, her chestnut brown hair spread out behind her. On either side of her body pools of blood soak the sheets. Her slit wrists are turned upward, a small silver dagger in her right hand.

My stomach turns and bile rises in my throat. I'm suddenly grateful I haven't eaten anything recently, or I'm sure it would be coming up right now. I stumble across her room, collapsing against the edge of her bed as the tears stream down my face. I reach out a shaking hand and stroke her cold face.

"No. No. No. No," I mumble. "You can't be dead. No!"

I shake my head.

"Did I do this to you? Is this my fault?"

I want her to wake up. I *need* her to wake up. Even if she slaps me. Even if she hates me. Even if she never wants to have anything to do with me ever again. I need her awake. I need her alive.

I grab her cold hand in mine. I don't even care about the sticky blood now staining my own hands.

"Wake up, Isabella," I plead. "I need you. I'm so sorry. I take it all back. I love you. I really do. Please, wake up. *Please.* I need you. I—"

I press my forehead to hers, sobs racking my body. I don't hear the door open, but I register the sound of footsteps just in time. I leap up from the bed. I look around desperately. I have to get out of here. There's an open balcony in her room. I quickly cross to it and hide behind the thick curtains billowing softly in the morning breeze. Footsteps enter the room, followed by a scream. I peek out from behind the curtain enough to see a maid standing just inside the door, her hands over her mouth and her eyes locked on Isabella in horror. A second maid comes rushing into the room.

"What's going on?" The second maid's eyes fall on the bed. "Oh heavens!" She makes a religious sign across her chest.

"We need to get her brother," the first maid says in a shaky voice. She turns to the second maid. "Do you know him?"

The maid nods, eyes wide. "Yes, he's with the prince. I'll get him. You stay here."

The second maid rushes from the room, and the other stares at Isabella for a moment, her shaking hands clutched together over her heart.

"Oh, child," she mutters. "What would make you do such a thing?"

Her voice is full of sadness and pity. It strikes chord in my heart, and I feel like I'm going to suffocate. I need to get out of here. I need to get away from the smell of blood. No, what I need is to wake up. This can't be real. It has to be another nightmare. I close my eyes as tight as I can, but when I open them I'm still in the room. Isabella is still dead.

Heavy bootsteps sound from the adjacent room, and my heart stops. Bram rushes into the room, Ehren at his heels, and halts in the doorway. His hand flies to his mouth and he sinks to his knees, unable to walk any further into the room.

"No," Ehren chokes, tears welling in his eyes. "No."

A tear slides free and my guilt increases.

"Bram . . . ," Ehren starts, placing his hand on Bram's shoulder.

Bram shakes it off, standing. He walks slowly toward the bed, shaking, tears on his cheeks.

"Oh, my sweet Isabella," he whispers. He reaches out and gently touches her hair. "Why did you have to follow me? Why didn't you stay home where you were safe? Why?"

"Who else has seen her?" Ehren asks the maid, his voice so quiet I barely hear him.

"Just me and Sadie, far as I know, Your Majesty," the maid whispers.

Ehren nods. "Keep this quiet. I want her buried respectably. Go fetch the death master. You know where to find him?" The maid nods. "Good. Now, go."

The maid scurries off, and Ehren approaches the bed and looks down. "Oh, Isabella."

I close my eyes. I've never felt pain like this. My own pain was bad enough, but now I feel like I have to bear the pain of Ehren and Bram. I need to get out of this room. I peer out from behind the curtain.

"I'll kill him," Bram growls, looking up at Ehren.

Ehren shakes his head in confusion. "Who?"

"Alak." Bram spits my name.

Gods, he knows. Somehow, he knows. I press my body flush against the wall. He cannot know I'm here.

"The rumors must have been true," Bram continues. "Alak really did trick her."

Ehren shakes his head. "I think he was sincere, Bram. I think this may be a misunderstand—"

"A misunderstanding?" Bram roars, his face red. "Does this look like a misunderstanding to you?"

"What do you want me to do?"

"I want Alak's head on a plate," Bram hisses. "I want him dead."

My heart stops.

"I will find him," Ehren promises, placing a hand on Bram's shoulder. "But now, we need to take care of Isabella."

Bram nods slowly. Then sobs rack his body once more, and he collapses against Ehren. Ehren holds his friend close, tears wetting his own cheeks.

They're not leaving any time soon, and if they find me here, they'll kill me. I have no doubt. It's no less than I deserve. Shaking, I slip out onto the balcony. I'm several stories up but this is my only means of escape. I look for a way down and notice a trellis just a few feet away. I climb up onto the balustrade and leap. My trembling fingers barely manage to grab the slots in the trellis. I slowly climb down, jumping the last few feet. I race to the stables as soon as my boots hit the ground. Mark greets me.

"Morning! Do you need your horse?"

I eye him nervously. How long before he hates me, too?

"Yes, please. Quickly."

Mark complies immediately, bringing Fawn out a couple minutes later, ready to go. I don't hesitate. I rush to mount her, eager to leave this all behind me. I try not to ride too quickly through the city—I don't want to draw attention to myself—but the moment I leave the gate, I make Fawn gallop as fast as she can. I need as much distance between me and the palace as I can get.

I ride all day, pushing Fawn as much as possible. Images of Isabella flash in my head as I ride, and tears flow down my cheeks until I have none left. I don't stop all day. I don't even stop when night falls. It's probably midnight before I finally bring Fawn to a halt, and it's only because she needs a break. I don't even try to sleep. I know I won't like my dreams. Once Fawn has had sufficient time to rest, we're back on the road. I don't push her quite as hard this time, but we keep a decent pace. I try to push away and bury my feelings. How often in life have I put on a false happy face? I can do it again. But every time I try to smile, I see Isabella's smile. And then that smile fades until her face is frozen in death.

Eventually, it all becomes too much. I stop Fawn. I collapse to the ground, curling up in a ball, tears somehow finding me again. My chest aches. I didn't realize hearts could literally break, but judging by the pain overwhelming me, mine must be truly broken. That is the only reason I could hurt this much. Death would be easier than feeling this.

Death. I should have just let Bram kill me. I deserve it.

Bram. I remember the dagger he gave me for my birthday. I have it with me, sheathed in my boot. I loose a long breath and pull out the dagger, the silver reflecting the light of the mid-morning sun. I turn my wrist upwards and place the cold blade against my skin.

"I'll be with you soon, Isabella," I whisper as I slice.

It stings, but the pain doesn't stop me from cutting the other wrist. I lay back in the grass on the side of the road as I feel life slowly draining away. I wonder who will find my body. Will anybody cry over me like they did Isabella? I can't imagine anyone will miss me. Hell, my death will be celebrated. They'll throw a parade in the streets, Bram and Ehren at the head. No one will mourn me. I close my eyes. Just a few more minutes and the pain will be gone. I start to fade. My time has come. Everything goes dark.

EIGHT

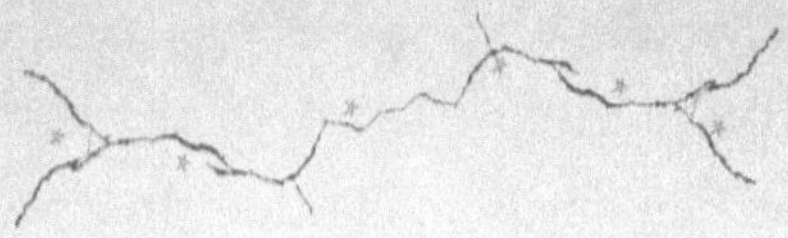

I smell meat roasting. My brain struggles to make sense of it. I should be dead. I want to be dead. I slowly open my eyes. It's night. A fire crackles nearby. I struggle to sit up, pain flashing from my wrists. I glance down to discover they've been tended to and wrapped in thick bandages.

"Careful now," a voice says. I look over and discover an older man crouching near a fire, turning an animal on a spit over the flames. "You nearly died."

I lie back down and stare up at the night sky. "I wanted to die."

"I gathered as much," the man muses. I realize he has an accent like mine. He's from Athiedor. "What can a young boy like you want to end his life over?"

"There's nothing left for me to live for."

"I disagree."

I turn my head and look at the man, scowling. "You don't know a thing about me."

"Hmmm," he says, turning the animal some more. "Perhaps not, but maybe I can guess a little. How does that sound?"

I look back up at the sky and sigh. "Guess away."

"All right, then. I say you've had a hard life. Harder than most. You lost your mother and your father at a relatively young age, but you're a survivor. You continued on when many would have given up."

I scoff. "You can easily make that up about anyone and have it be right."

"Oh, I'm not done. You've always thought yourself worthless and unwanted, until recently when you found people who accepted you as you were. You found friends. You cared for them, and they for you. You fell in love with a beautiful girl and gave your heart to her completely, but then some stupid fool messed it all up. Instead of staying and facing those you hurt, you ran. When the pain became too much, you tried to end it, but it's not your time. You still have purpose in this life, yet."

I sit up, ignoring the pain in my wrists, and stare at the man. His eyes twinkle in the firelight. There's something odd and off-putting about him.

"Are you a Seer?" I ask, then answer my own question, shaking my head. "No, that's not possible. Magic has been dead for centuries. Any Seers that exist only guess. You're just guessing."

He chuckles and shrugs. "Perhaps. Maybe I did just guess all those little details of your life. Maybe it was just luck I found you when I did. And it was even more luck that I happened to have the bandages and medicine needed to save your life. Maybe I'm lying when I tell you that you have a future. But, then again, maybe I know something you don't."

I study him for a moment. There's something about him. Something I can't quite place. His face is smug, like he really does know something I don't.

"Fine," I concede. "Tell me something about my future then. Prove to me I have something worth living for. Make me want to live."

The man grins. "Astra."

For reasons I don't understand, my heart stops and chills race across my skin.

"What? What does that even mean?"

"It's a name. Someone who will need you in the next few years. She'll depend on you and accept you without question, scars and all. And you'll love her more than you think possible."

I shake my head. "No. I've already met the love of my life and she's . . . she's gone. Forever. And it's my fault. I'll never love anyone like that again. You're wrong."

The man shrugs. "I've been wrong before, but this time, I don't think I am. You have a great purpose in this life. Your life hasn't been easy, and it won't be easy for the next several years. But you have a purpose. You just need to believe in yourself. The future needs you in it."

I shake my head and stare into the flames. "I don't believe you."

"Believe me or not, the twins will be of age in a few years, and everything will change. You need to be here when it happens."

I laugh bitterly. "The twins? They're a myth. Now I know you're crazy."

The man chuckles. "Believe as you wish, but I can assure you they are very much real. I've seen them with my own eyes."

I stare at him, my gaze steady and challenging. "And what do they have to do with me?"

"Only time will tell," he says, the twinkle returning to his eyes. "The question is, are you willing to live long enough to find out?"

I weigh his words. He's a crazy old man. He has to be. I look deep into his eyes. I can't shake the feeling that there's something more to him. But magic is dead. How can he know anything? Is he guessing? Is he lying? Surely he is. It's the only logical explanation. The only way for me to know for sure is to wait—to live. He's probably insane, but maybe, just maybe, he's right. Maybe I do have purpose. Maybe I do have a future. And that might be enough to live for.

ACKNOWLEDGMENTS

Wait. I have to write an acknowledgments page for each book? Oh well, here we go again, I suppose. *Gulps down some coffee*

The line up is essentially the same. I couldn't have gotten this far without family and close friends cheering me on. Special shoutouts go to my husband and my friend Lana. I'm glad you had your emotions destroyed along with me on those early drafts. Thanks also goes to Megan and Shanti for your feedback. You'll never know how much you helped make this book come to life.

This book was also largely a result of listening to the "Mad World" remix by Pentatonix, so I feel obligated to throw some credit their way. (Seriously, I listened to that song a near-endless loop for days while I wrote the first draft. Spotify was worried about me a bit.)

As always, thank you, the reader, for your support. I honestly wouldn't be where I am without you, and I'm glad we're on this journey together.

CONTENT WARNING INFORMATION

Physical Abuse/Assault

The story begins with a memory of the main character, Alak, being attacked and physically assaulted by his drunk father. During this encounter, Alak defends himself and ends up killing his abuser.

Suicide

This story deals heavily with the theme of suicide, focussing the events in the last two portions of the story. One character is discovered in her bed after the act and another character attempts suicide shortly after. The first suicide happens off-page, but the second does not. The second attempt is not successful and the character decides that life is worth living after all.

US National Suicide Prevention Hotline: 1-800-273-8255

*UK National Suicide Prevention Hotline: 0800
689 5652*

*Canada Suicide Prevention Service Call: 1-
833-456-4566*
Canada Suicide Prevention Service Text: 45645

*Australia Suicide Callback Service: 1300
659 467*
*Talk Suicide: https://suicidepreventionpathways.
org.au/make-a-referral*

Additional Details

This story also deals with general trauma from growing up with an abuser, killing in self-defense, and slight themes of depression and feeling unworthy and unloved.

ABOUT THE AUTHOR

AMBER D LEWIS is a new adult fantasy author with a Bachelor's Degree in Publishing. She currently lives in Taylors, SC with her husband and three kids. When she's not reading or writing books, you'll probably find her wandering the aisles of Target.

The *Fire and Starlight Saga* is her first published collection, but she plans on sharing many more stories.